MANY LIBRARIES IN ESSEX HAVE
FACILITIES FOR EXHIBITIONS AND
MEETINGS — ENQUIRE AT YOUR
LOCAL LIBRARY FOR DETAILS

GW00642264

30130 13

Shadow of the Sun

MAI ZETTERLING

Shadow
of the Sun

JONATHAN CAPE
THIRTY BEDFORD SQUARE LONDON

FIRST PUBLISHED 1974
© 1974 BY MAI ZETTERLING

JONATHAN CAPE LTD, 30 BEDFORD SQUARE, LONDON WCI

ISBN 0 224 01038 7

PRINTED BY BUTLER & TANNER LTD, FROME AND LONDON

Contents

For Marianne

One

]1[

Dear, good brother,

I have just torn another useless day from my wall almanack and tomorrow stares me in the face in the shape of Friday the 13th. I feel gloomy about its prospects. I keep repeating one question to myself—what the hell am I doing running around like some Japanese dancing-mouse, up and down the same steps, streets, corridors?

Never mind, for the moment I'm doing what I'm told because I'm still quite stunned by my prompt job-offers after twenty years of absence. To be able to choose between the stuffy right-wing papers and the harmless so-called Left is for me of course a great boost at just the moment when I needed it most. So you are quite right to say, which you would, Good God, girl, you ought to be celebrating, and so I am at the very moment with a plain omelette and a bottle of cheap vino tinto. It's a far cry from the truffle omelette and the Meursault it would undoubtedly have been in Buenos Aires, but of course I don't miss it in the least. I'd much rather sit here alone at a messy table with pans, bread-crumbs, typewriter and thumbed manuscript than have the polished table, the starched napkins, the docile servants and Eric's hostile face around and about me.

Yes, there are good reasons for celebrating all that, and why I still feel low in spirit is quite easy to figure out. For the most part it's Eric, poor, sad, half-cracked man—how can you live with somebody like that without losing your own wits? He hasn't stopped ringing since I arrived here—that's money for you—and he certainly doesn't bother to find out the time difference between Sweden and Argentina. Anyway, it suits him to wake me in the middle of the night; he knows that the vulnerability of the dark and the helplessness one feels after totally meaningless curses and accusations is loneliness complete. And it's very frustrating for me as he never answers a question about the children and his way of torturing me gets worse when he has been drinking, which these days is pretty often. So that's number one of the spirit dampeners.

Number two is that although I like my new-found position in life, the authority it gives, etc., I'm employed in a large concern which basically doesn't give a damn and which like most newspapers, however enlightened, is still corrupt, attuned to gossip, death, sensation and negativism. And I'm expected to deal in all four with wit, vehemence and sarcasm. Not exactly uplifting and certainly not like working for the *Christian Science Monitor,* which might have been a better idea on the whole.

Number three is my concern about you, dear Teddy, the fact that you're so far away, the headaches, the spine trouble. Do you want me to find out what they do here for your particular problem? At least I'm in the right place—people really seem frightened of dying here more than anywhere I know, except when they drown their melancholy in wood alcohol and then cut their wrists in some sort of northern stupor.

After all these reasons for being listless and lonely at times, I shall tell you now about the better things that have happened and are happening. From time to time you've accused me, quite rightly, of being unfair to our country; I couldn't even see the beauty of it except in the basic touristic charms of a town with bridges and water and well-planned parks. My eyes this spring seem to have been new born, but I can't help seeing in the same way the old streets we used to tramp those hot miserable summers. They will never change.

On the other hand new things seem to happen to old buildings, as when the sun hits them and they burn saffron and turn
terracotta, and I find the boisterous happy icy water such a
funny contrast to people's solemn faces that I want to giggle,
and I've discovered little nooks above the city, cobbled court-
yards with lovely old water-pumps that would make a scrap-
dealer's heart thump with joy, rows of outhouses, wood-smoke
lingering, flowers in such profusion that it makes sense of
butterflies and the winged pollinators.

But because I'm dealing with odds and ends all over the city,
I come upon every quarrel we ever had during those seemingly
so endless days. Were we bored? I'm sorry on thinking back
what bad company I was for you then—as I remember, I could
see no joy anywhere and was teenagerly sullen. But those three
summers can never be forgotten. Time has kept them sacred
for me—our sad little games of never stopping on the joins
of the paving-stones or counting to a certain number before
reaching the end of the street. And all the penalties we thought
up. There you had the upper hand, I must say.

You remember? Which reminds me to tell you of the curious
woman I've seen several times pacing up and down the street,
who seems to be playing some similar game with herself ... But
that will just have to wait—it's late. I will draw the blinds, put
my ear-mufflers and my pirate's eyeband on, take a couple of
sleeping-pills, try to make my mind a blank and hope to sink
into a deep oblivion without any dreams.

Dear receptacle, dear brother, dear Teddy, another report
soon. Meanwhile here is as much love as I can possibly muster
at the time for you and you only, and I do want to hear more of
what you're doing about your ills. That's what is urgent and all-
important. Anything else can wait.

]2[

Cher frère,

I shall certainly do my very best to keep this summer calm and clean and if possible happy. Do you know, I realize that for years this little simple word had gone right out of my head and when I practised saying it to myself the other day it left a funny taste in the mouth, burned my tongue almost. Happiness, serenity, peace, yes, I need a long draught of it all to get together everything that's me, or was me, into decent shape again.

I keep my self-respect going by being extraordinarily well-groomed on the outside to fool my bosses and so-called friends, because if they caught one glimpse of the chaos within they would run away screaming. I suppose what I long for most is smiling happy faces and I've certainly come to the wrong place for that—should have gone to a sunny spaghetti-land and had my bum nipped by oily gents. I'm sure that would have done me a world of good, but we are a long way from that kind of open frivolity here.

Oh dear, where are the smiling faces? The tight masks have been too close for too long, certainly including my own frightened visage which I look at in horror every morning. No, I must make a giant effort to start afresh with as few prejudices as possible and believe in myself and the world again.

But perhaps there are too many skeletons in the closet? I don't like thinking about my planned accident, all so desperately wrong, ill-conceived, cowardly and selfish. I bow my head in shame and turn my thoughts towards hope and think of you.

Apart from work, you ask, what's my social world? Well, except for other similarly freaky journalists and a few notabilities again vaguely connected with work, I don't see anyone.

The supposed 'friends' seem so very long ago, and so much has happened to both them and me, that I feel tired even contemplating steps to recover the sort of lost childhood it seems to be. After all, they were all more or less connected with school, a few with newspapers — in any case, they all seem to have disappeared, died of boredom perhaps, I haven't bothered to find out.

As you must have gathered, I'm too exhausted emotionally to face anything highly personal. As for a lover, my insides are so many rags and tatters, a patchwork of garish emotions, and it just wouldn't be fair, for however short a time, to let anyone in. Also I don't believe sex would be that interesting and I still have too much respect and a vivid memory of how gloriously good it can be. So for the present it's a very closed shop, although I have my randy moods when I cast my eye round the possibilities, which are, I assure you, very few. I'm still making too many comparisons. I suppose that's a curse we'll have to accept for the rest of our lives, n'est-ce pas?

I promised to tell you about that oddity of a woman whom I see around town almost every day. She really does pace the street. I can't at all figure out what she is up to. She chooses a bit of pavement, then remains in this self-inflicted space and takes so many steps back and forth within it. It's amazing what force she puts into every one of those steps across her little area of no more than six metres. It seems her whole body is pressing into the ground and I'm always surprised not to see her footprints on the pavement. She never steps on the dividing-lines, always puts her foot firmly down in the middle, thus reminding me of our childish games.

So there she is, arms hanging limply on each side, face down. I've never seen her eyes and don't really know what she looks like — it's just her rigid, heavy walk reminiscent of a wild animal in a cage, back and forth ten times, then a very sudden change in movement and attitude: stops, stands transfixed, there's a tremendous tension around her, then an odd jerky lift of both arms over her head, the slightest of hesitations, you can feel the strain, eyes still firmly fixed on the ground, then a violent downward movement with both arms, and she is all spent, it seems—if it weren't for the fact that she then starts all over again. I get exhausted just thinking about it.

She disturbs me deeply and I can't explain why. I feel both fear and a certain embarrassment. I can feel the effect she has on other people pretending not to notice her. She fascinates me. I want to find out more, but then I never do. But she stirs up trouble in my soul, gives out vibrations that somehow seem close to my unconscious. The odd thing is that I never seem to look at her squarely, only out of the corner of my eye, as if scared of too close a contact with some insanity which is within us all and too easy to slip into. She has planted herself very strongly on my horizon.

Otherwise today has been the usual mess, a quarrel with the editor, a squabble over photographs, misunderstanding with almost everyone. Does one really speak the same language? I have done my usual little dancing-mouse trick, round and round the same faces, places, meetings, canteens, and have survived another day on bad nourishment. It all seems fatty and absolutely without taste and I eat joylessly and that infuriates me. Do you remember the sensual meals we used to make while Mother was at work? I would love to get back that roaring appetite for life.

Tomorrow I shall put my hair-piece on, my best strand of pearls almost choking me, be spotless and well-pressed, behave like a very good girl, and give the photographers my best grinning teeth. It's for the première of a new Swedish musical, and your reviewer has got her seat with the lions and will behave accordingly. She knows how to play the game to survive. They haven't got a clue how frail the art-work is. The slightest ripple would tear apart the finery.

The funny thing is I'm doing it so well that I have succeeded in getting myself a name as one of the toughest critics of the human scene. Her vitriolic pen, etc ... There seems to be both respect and fear in their appreciation, even from the editor himself. I'm getting a fantastic amount of extra work at the moment—well-paid too, so from that point of view I'm not complaining.

I won't bother to tell you the latest of Eric. It's such a repetitive business. Sometimes I wish he would have a little more imagination. Poor man, he really is frightfully boring, both to himself and to his surroundings. But of course he can wear one out with that tedious insistence of his.

You say nothing of your ills. I wish you would. Our blood-brotherhood pact still holds, I hope. All or nothing. So do tell me please. Also I wish you would find your work less irksome. Do you really have to do it much longer, when you certainly don't need it for the money? What about the house in the mountains waiting for you? Do you ever see it? It must be lonely for it there without you.

]3[

Lovely Teddy,

I'm in the midst of writing a so-called witty review and I despair, so have taken a moment off with you, however pressing time is, five hours left and nothing yet on paper.

At the moment I want to resort to infantilism, because I feel insulted. I would like to invent a whole new language of grunts and groans, spits and gurgles, but perhaps the only correct review, which would display a lively style if not exactly the best of taste, would be to let my knickers down in public and give a resounding fart which would blow the roof off the theatre.

The most insulting thing, I suppose, is that the private parts all over the place and the four-letter words used so often and so vehemently are somehow involved in left-wing politics and social justice. The trouble is you hear the familiar words but not the important message which is being shouted without talent. But enough—I must think of something else.

I think I forgot to tell you what my wandering, lost person looks like, always dressed the same way, no matter what the weather, in an oddly timeless costume—a brown beret with the sweat-band pulled down over her forehead, thick ankle-socks and once-white plimsolls, a longish brown raincoat with large lapels and tightly belted by a long gay scarf, and always gloves of a nondescript colour. I saw her again from the taxi as I went to the theatre: strange that she keeps cropping up as she does. I feel I don't do her justice in describing her. There is something so haunting there. She seems more real than anything I have ever seen and at the same time like a ghost from lands we can't even begin to comprehend.

Several hours later. The streets are heaving away under my window, monsters are at work swallowing garbage. The noise is in my head, I seem to be chewing those beer-cans, crunch, crunch. I have guilt feelings about the dentist, I always postpone my dates with him. I look dreadful, strained, pasty-faced, a poor little rabbit-head. Now the lift has started its morning routine as well and the door slams viciously in the corridor. Sometimes in my more neurotic moods I really feel persecuted by my neighbours.

A lot seems to have happened since I stopped writing five hours ago. Eric rang in one of his more nauseating states—as if I hadn't had enough filth for one evening, he heaped it on me until I couldn't take it any more, so I hung up, pulled the plug out, had a whisky, had a bit of a cry, another whisky, wrote a few unpublishable lines, tore them up, started feeling guilty, put the plug back in again, began a clean page, and once more my pen seemed to run out of ink when the telephone rang again. He was in the opposite mood this time, cringing and sorry for himself. I don't know which I find more despicable.

Anyway, my emotions got dreadfully mixed up. I have become an expert in self-hatred and have found it very expensive. The psychiatrist I visit twice a week tries to sort out my sad, neglected inner person. It's a relief, so for the moment I'll continue, and I do seem to be in great company—he is more heavily booked than any ordinary doctor. So where are all the healthy Swedes we hear so much about? Eating nuts and berries, sunbathing in the raw, scalding themselves in saunas and getting chilblains from frozen lakes, I suppose. We are a mad nation and I was as mad as a hatter when I married Eric.

But he seemed to be very normal at first, behaving impeccably in every new situation, even in bed. I was totally fooled like everyone else. In my present job I come across many oddities and keep pinching myself to make sure I'm awake, because there are times when I say under my breath, 'No, this one is really going too far, nobody behaves like that,' but then of course I need only think back to Eric and I don't know whether to cry or laugh. What with me in choirboy outfits, the heavy incensed bedrooms and all the toys on the floor, he literally used to drool over the little fire-engines and ambulances. It was indeed pathetic and he was finally happy because he had let me into his secret world—the only one he had, I think.

When I realized there were deeper problems, such as boys, I even became panicky for Paul, but I suppose it never occurred to him to assault his own son—though he adored him, as you saw for yourself, and poor Estelle was left very much in the background. Little did anyone know of the monsters he kept in check. Perhaps it was because of that house where he was brought up, guarded like a prison on account of the valuables it contained. I'll never forget the high walls, the men with guns, the dogs let loose at night, the icy unfriendliness where there were only deals and money to discuss. So I still say—poor Eric. But again he was lucky to be in Argentina and in his elevated position when they found him out—otherwise he'd have done a reasonably long sentence.

Dear, my pen has the dancing sickness, it seems—can't stop,

B

though I'm really tired now. I have put the kindly ear-plugs in, so now it's beautifully blissfully quiet at last, but it still hurts to look outside, so I'll put the whole night uniform on with the eye-pieces and I shall sleep. The only thing I'm not looking forward to is that beastly operator who will ring in a couple of hours and ask me who I am and what my number is. I expect I shall soon have to reveal to her my income-tax returns, my menstrual days, my sex life, my bank statement. She is so damned official. Once when I tried to break down the barrier and say something humorous, she cut me off with 'There's no time to talk', in an if possible even icier tone.

]4[

My dear so much better half,

There she was on the pavements again, for the first time in my seedy district, only a few streets from where I live. She was pacing just opposite the bus-stop, so I had a good chance to take a long look at her. Nothing had changed in her appearance, her movements back and forth. She was as powerful as ever. I suddenly remembered the camera in my satchel, the Nikon with the long lens and, not feeling in the least shy of spying on her, I found her easy to follow as I know so well her patterns of movement, and I came quite close to those birdlike features. But I still couldn't get a glimpse of her eyes.

The colour of her hair surprised me. Most of it was tucked under the beret, but the tufts she hadn't managed to hide were of a stringy straw-like texture tinged with bright yellow and green — yes, I did think for a moment that something had gone wrong with my eyesight. Her age is difficult to guess, there are no lines on her face — but she must be around thirty-five, perhaps more. Her ears were standing out from her head like a pixie.

And all of a sudden I found myself taking a picture of her. I hadn't meant to do it but there my finger was, on the button, which clicked. I felt a shiver down my spine as if I had touched her and for the first time I noticed a new response in her to the world around, as if she had been woken up. That private aloofness was gone for some seconds. She stopped and looked up at the sky and seemed to shiver, and her eyes were shining saucers, that's all I can say. They stopped me in my tracks and I hardly realized that the bus was arriving. As I stepped into it, things had returned to normal again, but as I sat down disturbed, bewildered—yes, I had to admit that something really had happened to me, and she was just the same, pacing to and fro with arms dangling.

This experience has made me uneasy all day and I wish I could forget her as readily as the rest of the world obviously can. Nobody cares, nobody does anything to change her pattern. So why should this happen to me just now? I don't want any part in it. I smell trouble and I say no. No—go away, little woman, play your games on someone else's pavement. Yet the whole thing is strangely persistent.

Home again after a fairly long and hectic day, what do I do? I put on a sixteenth-century piece of music to deaden the smells of the yellow, oh so very yellow, fatty pea-soup that penetrates every wall of the building. I give myself treats. I pour exquisite perfume over my neck. I eat Danish caviare for the lack of the real thing, swill cold white wine down the gullet, take a hot bath, black coffee, cigarettes. I'm pretending to live and be my sensual self again, which seems light-years away.

But as I'm in a complex mood not even the loudest harpsichord can drown the slurps, gurgles and burps that I seem to have in my eardrums. I'm back to that yellow pea-soup again. Hundreds seem to be drinking it. It's amazing how the smell even sticks to clothes as I hurry down the corridor with key poised towards my door—they have taken on the fatty odour and in my mind turned everything the colour of sulphur. I know it spells childhood and misery, but that knowledge doesn't seem to help at all.

The rats in my upper storey are not very kind to me, but I suppose a long illness, which is the only way to describe my last few years, colours everything and it takes time, as the text-books say, to be healed, to recover, to be close to oneself again. Work is the best deadener for the moment—it keeps most of the ghosts away—so I accept far too much of it, since I don't dare to take the spaces in between. Because of this ferocious pace, prospects are good—journalism, translations, radio talks, the lot. I might even move to a friendlier flat with no smells, where I can rest my eyes on trees, imagine they are jungles and try to picture you walking through them. I can't for the life of me put you into what I see from this window—other stagnant living-rooms where people pass to and fro, making patterns that I don't understand.

By the way I have a theory about these vacant faces. Television has cast the blue light on them for too long, it's like the dangers of too much X-ray treatment. As I'm the only one who knows this, I have a duty to take it to the authorities and make them stop television altogether to see the effect—or has the disease gone too far already like a cancer in the bones?

Dear Teddy, enough of fantasy for one night. Eyes are smarting from looking at too many dictionaries, as I've been working on my Spanish translation. And while this tiredness persists I shall with the utmost speed take myself to bed and hope not to be woken up by another call from Eric. I love you dearly and kiss your noble forehead.

]5[

Queridísimo Hermano,

Haven't written to you for days because I've been in the north and talked to miners, as there is trouble stirring up there; and

they have my full support. The miners themselves are handsome
brutes in comparison with the usual pasty-faced male Swede
and it seems they have some guts left. I will send you my
article. But oh dear, your sister behaved in just the way she
had promised herself not to.

After a dreary hotel dinner, starting with the customary
three sandwiches, and with the customary bit too much to
drink—they eat early up here—there was the whole evening
left for making notes. So feeling randy (those damn miners, I
suppose), well, I couldn't very well go out on the streets and
get one, so I had—or, rather, still have—a messy affair with
this young, curly-headed photographer, sweet-faced, opinion-
ated and a bit scared of me but not wanting to admit it. He has
now become my slave. But I don't want it, so I'm in the process
of clearing it all up. Foolish woman.

When I came back home though, what joy! A thick bundle
through the Embassy from you. It was suddenly Christmas, our
birthday, you name it. I sat myself down in a sunny spot,
opened a new packet of cigarettes, had a cup of coffee, put my
feet up and celebrated, went through every emotion I'm
capable of, fury about Bertha, pleasure from the photographs,
happiness about your health, and of course ecstasy over your
feelings about us, however disturbing it is.

I'm not saying a word about Bertha. How can I, silly man?
I'm so biased. I don't want in any way to influence you.
Mustn't. If things have come to this unbearable pass you will
have to solve it sooner or later in some fashion—and it has to
be your fashion. The worry about the children is more than
understandable, though just one thing—don't do what most
men in your situation do and wait until it's too late for the
woman to start a new life. It's more cruel to leave when the
children do. Perhaps you yourself would feel less guilty having
done your bit. For almost any man there's a teenager waiting,
but for a middle-aged woman—nothing. Especially if, like
Bertha, she has nothing but a home life to fall back on. That's
my only advice.

I know for myself that at the age of forty I'm well-preserved, as they say—but take care, frightened as a bloody rabbit: the diet, the weekly sauna, the hairdresser, the manicurist, and I hate it, and I know the day will come when all that will go and I shall dare to face anyone without disguise, and I'm working towards it consciously. Afraid Bertha wouldn't have a clue what I'm talking about. But I feel what you are going through, if for no other reason than because of our twinship. Most of the time it is a blessing, but it can also be a great nuisance. What we need for both of us to feel good is to live very sedate little lives. I certainly don't want you to suffer even the slightest of my agonies. You say, what can we do but live together? I'm not ready yet, the thought still scares me, as you know ...

I stopped, because Eric of course rang—so did the young photographer, both pleading. I felt cruel, so slept uneasily, tossing as in a storm, had two disturbing dreams. I was invited by a very dubious person for a lift in a straw basket with a lot of other people all dressed up as for carnival—except the woman pacer, who was looking the same as ever in beret and raincoat. The basket was fastened to some sort of line on a high pole. We took off at lightning speed, whizzing through the air into open countryside. Suddenly I see a small hole in the earth and through this we go, down and down into a wonderland with the most exotic and stylized groupings of tropical trees and flowers. I imagine it looks a bit like that where you are now. We play childish games and the woman becomes animated, even happy.

In the other dream I'm making revolutionary posters. I share a seedy flat with several people. I'm on a rooftop. A demonstration will take place in the street, a band marches by and everything has turned sepia. I'm lying in a precarious position, very frightened, I start sobbing. I turn to look for someone and I see the woman again. I ask her to hold my hand as I shift into a safer position, I'm scared of trying it on my own. After changing, I once more turn to look for her, but now she has a plastic mask over her face. She looks hideous and I plead with her to take it off. I'm still sobbing when I wake up, apparently unable to stop it as I live on in a dream world, yet wide awake.

The night was destroyed, and finally I pulled myself together and sat down to work. But that woman kept on interfering with my concentration. I hope she's not going to be my nightly guest, as I get quite enough of her during the day when I jump grasshopper fashion all over the town. I don't know how she manages it — I take buses, undergrounds, taxis, but she has only her two feet. I'm expecting to see scars wherever she has trampled and left traces of her agonized emotions. I wish she would let me alone.

]6[

My dear alter ego,

Because of a chance happening I now know all about her. It was last Saturday evening with a feeling of anticipation in the air, a complete change of atmosphere. The town was ready to be ambushed, insulted, abused and invaded. So were the police, with whom I had made a rendezvous for a number of articles to be written on youth, drugs, alcohol and the whole, by now uninteresting, overwritten problem. It was one of those flowery nights on which all seems suddenly to have come out in bloom and you are hit by perfumes from every direction — such clarity of sky, a night to be spent in the open, made for love, for beautiful thoughts. Instead I was to spend most of it in the back of a police van.

I felt ill at ease from the start. Although the van seemed immaculately clean, as everything in this country is, it had a curious odour hard to define but which I later diagnosed as vomit, liquor and an intermittent emotional charge it had stored up. It made me nervous. The policemen themselves were gentlemanly, slightly flattered, nice enough I suppose, but with the wrong sort of niceness, and of course I've never taken to men in uniforms. No, I certainly wasn't happy, but I was doing a job.

They knew what I was looking for and were eager to supply it. I could hear them arguing among themselves about the places and the timing. Catching drunken drivers was the first stage and I sat mesmerized, trying to keep calm and detached; then came the tours of the parks with the dogs, finding old, forlorn men in hedges or sliding off benches with empty bottles in empty portfolios and alone. The third place was full of haggard Lolitas with tough accents and dirty vocabularies, offering a quiet resistance to plain-clothes policemen and social workers, evangelists intermingling, interfering gently. And drugs were found.

And people were stowed away behind me, with only a metal bar between us and no human contact, only sullen eyes—and I felt a sickness welling up inside, a real childish tummy-ache, and I started to shiver and sweat at the same time, and in front of the royal castle I had to ask them to stop. I fell out of the van and was as sick as I can ever remember into the swirling waters. A gallant policeman held my forehead as a mother would and gave me his handkerchief. And as I lay there heaving, the whole sordid affair of Eric's with the gardener's two small boys came back with a tremendous force: the look of greed on the faces of both the father and the chief of police when they had been given the hush money, that very father who at first had been beside himself with worry.

There was no way of explaining—I had merely got sick all of a sudden. Could they take me home please? I felt their disappointment; they obviously thought the night was still full of promise. I was sitting in front between two broad-shouldered epaulettes feeling small and fragile on the way home. They didn't seem to notice the stupidly beautiful things we passed, rose-coloured walls, buildings that seemed to sway and move, the sharp glimmer in a window reflecting water and the dawn

sun. I said something feeble about how rather nice it all looked
and wished I hadn't. All I got back was a quick glance and an
irritated yawn.

The police radio had been busy all along, but a new excitement had crept into their code language and looks of con-
spiracy passed over my head. We were by a harbour of small
boats, we passed a staggering figure, a kind of contortionist
made of rubber by the look of his walk, but they didn't stop or
even notice him, but swung into a small alley with a suddenness
that made me realize that something was going to happen. They
apologized hurriedly, but they had received orders to run to
earth a group of addicts.

They found them, human debris wrapped in newspapers, tied
up with string, heads and feet in boxes against the still cold and
damp nights: expressionless grey faces, bewildered animals.
Used to the pushing and dragging, there wasn't a murmur from
one of them. The police had arrived in force—they were all
over the place, working with silent brutality. I didn't feel real.
And I wanted to break down and cry when I saw *her*.

I had wandered a bit away on the quay and was staring into
the rippled waters in my half despair, when I shifted my glance
to a boat where the police were making their next search. She
hadn't protected herself like the others, just laid her body out
on the bare boards. She seemed to have shrunk. I found myself
helping to carry her to the van and then with sirens blaring we
cut through the streets. Panic in the air was all we left
behind.

I didn't question anything as I sat with her head in my lap
and my hands over hers trying to give some warmth. And
finally I was alone with her in an echoing waiting-room in a
hospital and it was the most natural thing in the world, don't
ask me why.

That her name was Larsson and her first name Anne-Marie
was something of a shock. It didn't fit in with my picture of her.
But yes, they knew her all right. This was the mental ward of a
large hospital. From time to time she gave herself voluntarily to

them. Sometimes she would be picked up by the police and delivered, a half-dead bundle in a coma. What was new this time was that they had found needle-marks in her arm.

They took my name and address, as if it would help. I was too tired to explain anything—anyway what could I explain? I saw her body on a stretcher swallowed up by the innards of the hospital. She had a mother and a sister, who now arrived like a couple of dormice and I couldn't help taking over the situation. They were embarrassed and apologetic to everyone with their timid smiles, so I found myself making all the arrangements, and in the taxi they were full of gratitude and please would I at least come in for a cup of coffee? By this time I needed it. I accepted.

The thought of her, or rather this new person called Anne-Marie, among the sterile dainty Meissen shepherdesses and frilly Spanish dancing-girls which were dotted on every available space, was to say the least strange. Painted velvet cushions, porcelain ducks flying in formation on the wall, starched lace curtains, heavy antiques, armchairs from the 'thirties, the best modern Danish tables, all intermingling; double windows still in place, central heating going strong; life seemed remote. Not a sound from outside, although I knew the street to contain a certain amount of traffic even on a Sunday morning.

Embroidered serviettes. Porcelain cups with yellow roses. Dainty home-made canapés. Weak coffee. And Mrs Larsson smiled, bowed, tripped around making little noises. She was behaving like a passé air-hostess and I felt very much like a passenger—not to be allowed out of the seat until I reached my destination, and it was absolutely up to Mrs Larsson to decide when that moment came. I had to accept it all.

This then is the picture. I sank into the comfortable armchair slowly being hypnotized by Mrs Larsson busybodying on tiptoe with her coffee arrangements. And there was Barbro, the sister, staring out of the window, looking for her future, who knows what, heavily built, white-faced, with a tight perm, little sausages of curls. Early forties, I suppose, but too many wrinkles and lines of bitterness. She was wearing the most unbecoming, outmoded clothes — for that matter they both seemed to belong to another time. The mother was more her own age, sixty or so, with quite a neat figure, a rosy complexion of sorts, her streaky grey hair pushed tidily back into a bun. It was a kindly face, but totally nondescript, just as Barbro's was blank and lifeless. She was gentle in her manners and had a low voice which apologized for itself.

She had been left by a husband when the girls were in their teens. She had been quite happy; they had never got on well. There was no bitterness or sentiments, she was just stating facts. Nobody had missed him. This house and three others in the same street were an inheritance, so she was completely in charge after he left. That she should have found this difficult didn't surprise me, but what did was the fact that the girls together took over all business dealings on her behalf and made themselves indispensable. I gathered it had been a happy time with the three of them cosily tucked up in their comforts, caring only about one another. There seemed to have been no close friends except a couple of elderly aunts whom they saw from time to time and a cousin from the north, who had lodged with them for a while.

Now and then I felt a certain impatience from the window where Barbro was still sitting. When Anne-Marie's name was mentioned, sighs could be heard. Yes, extraordinary how two children from the same parents could be so very different. There was Barbro, a normal baby, who always did well at school, never any trouble, tidy, obedient, the perfect daughter. But from the very start there was something odd about Anne-Marie; even the nurses had noticed it.

She had never cried as a baby. Doctors were consulted about it and they laughed. The mother ought to be grateful, they had said, but she couldn't help feeling it was unnatural. Then as soon as the girl started to talk, she preferred speaking to animals and plants or for that matter any kind of inanimate object. They were all amused at first, but when she persisted it became an embarrassment. Doctors were again consulted with no other result than that she stopped talking thus in front of them. But as soon as she was left alone they could hear her talking non-stop to everything around her.

They had to admit, however, that she had an almost electric effect on plants and animals. Dogs would leave their masters and literally crawl towards her and lick her legs and whimper. Cats came from nowhere when she sat on a bench in the park. Small children adored her. Her potted plants were almost a joke; she had the greenest fingers they had ever known.

In school she was a misfit, adored, feared, mocked. There was a barrier between her and the other children – she lived in a country of her own which they had no access. She never seemed to mind. She walked a curious tight-rope; living entirely in her fantasy world she could cope with school, but of course without prizes, unlike Barbro who always came out on top.

Anne-Marie took over the dealings with people while Barbro did the books. Then the cousin turned up, a gentle character in his early thirties, who had been moved down to the Stockholm office. He was biding his time with them until a flat became vacant in one of Mrs Larsson's houses. They liked having him there and at first he treated the girls as children, giving them Easter eggs, taking them for outings, communal singing in the open air, boat-rides in the summer, Christmas markets, even to a restaurant. But he had also taken them to the Salvation Army, in which he was a Captain, and this Mrs Larsson didn't like one bit.

She wasn't religious herself and of course didn't mind if people went to church on Sundays, but the Army was different, there was something funny about it. And as for singing at street corners in their uniforms and beating those drums, well, she felt it was most embarrassing. And he was proud of it. He also used to sell the newspaper in his spare time and that surely was not the sort of thing a grown-up man should do. He always talked of God as if he knew him personally.

Mrs Larsson had tried to shut her ears to such talk. Barbro shared her feelings. But Anne-Marie had devoured it from the start and was soon deeply involved. She blamed Arne for it, but said nothing; she tried to talk sense to Anne-Marie, but got nowhere.

Then Arne asked for Anne-Marie's hand in marriage.

Mrs Larsson had had no idea of the growing love between them and at once burst into tears. No, no, she didn't mind that the girl was to be taken away from her, she didn't even mind the Army—no, no, and he was decent, gentle, even charming, with good prospects. But they were cousins—that surely must be wrong. Finally, very disturbed, she went to the priest to talk it over. She must stop the marriage. But despite meetings in the church and at home with all present, Arne had made up his mind—and so for that matter had Anne-Marie.

An album was placed in front of me, a heavy leather-bound book with every picture neatly labelled by Mrs Larsson or Barbro. Noticing the full ash-tray and realizing the coffee was cold, they went to make more and left me alone. I felt a certain shame sitting there, I felt I was being told too much. I wanted to leave, but at the same time couldn't. I found myself staring out of the same window as Barbro, not so much looking out as looking inside myself, and I thought of you, of us, brother and sister just couldn't be allowed to marry and have children, it was a crime in the eyes of the world.

We suffered guilt and anxiety about our love from the very first, what could we do but hide it, keep it to ourselves? So what then did we do out of fear? We committed two crimes, two lousy marriages that produced children we never deeply cared for, though we have never stopped being consumed by our love for each other. I know it was always you who pleaded with me to accept the fact and damn the world. I'm coming closer to you all the time now. It's beginning to make sense.

]7[

So there I was in the summer of 1963 with another Anne-Marie
smiling shyly into the camera. The face was neither handsome
nor ugly, but it was a kind of haunting, shining face, the kind
that angels ought to wear. Anne-Marie sitting with Arne
against a backdrop of lilacs, her eyes luminous, so obviously in
love with him, though he slightly disappointed me — tall, gentle,
yes, high forehead, a bit of a squint, he looked solid and boring,
but there was also a steely look that disturbed me about him, I
don't know why. Then 'Summer '64 the Island' — and there
again is Anne-Marie with a very large seagull in her lap and
grinning hysterically into the lens. Now this picture really gets
me worried for no apparent reason, but at that moment Mrs
Larsson appears with more refreshments and I drink the hot
coffee that I don't really want and nibble at the cakes and open
yet another packet of cigarettes.

The sun danced on the walls, it was nearing midday, the
room was unbearably hot. I wanted them to fling open the
windows, felt almost feverish in my need for air, yet I sat there
helplessly with nothing more to say. I had become a receptacle
for Mrs Larsson to fill, nothing could stop her now, there was
no reluctance left, the sentences flowed more freely. She had
almost forgotten herself in her eagerness to tell all.

Somewhat craftily she had arranged the wedding for one
year ahead, hoping for a miracle or a change of heart. What
actually happened was something she could never have guessed
in her wildest dreams.

Telephone calls from girls began. Voices vaguely familiar.
Always asking for Arne when he couldn't or shouldn't have
been there. Giggly voices as if at a party, making suggestions
that disturbed Mrs Larsson. But she neither wanted nor dared

to take them seriously, they were too impertinent, too far removed from her own life. But when they persisted for months, she began halfheartedly to write down the names and addresses she was given of girls whom Arne was supposed to visit instead of doing his good works at the Army.

Out of curiosity she tried one of the numbers and the girl answered. On another occasion it was Arne himself who picked up the telephone. It was uncanny and she kept it to herself, which was how she came to spy on him against her will. She trembled at the thought, yet had to do it.

One dismal greyish day she found herself in a doorway on a back street. She waited, not believing anything would happen, in a sort of cold stupor, somehow doing her duty and feeling as numb and grey as the day itself. Then, as in a bad dream, she saw a blind pulled up, a window opened, and there he was, in shirtsleeves, dishevelled, looking quite different from his normal daily self. Later they came out together, she a young thing clinging to his arm, they glanced quickly round but missed her, standing like a stone figure in the opposite doorway, then exchanged kisses before parting. And then she followed him. She followed him without a thought of what the future would bring. She was trembling and weak at the knees, yet she could not stop.

He was on his way home, but taking it easy—looking in windows, buying a paper and finally sitting down in a café. She faltered, not knowing what she was doing, then took a seat some tables away from him. For a long time they sat, he absorbed in the newspaper, she not touching the coffee she had ordered, wondering what would happen next. Vaguely she thought how silly it was—now she had proof she didn't know what to do with it. She ought to have planned it better.

Then he looked up, for a split-second guilt was all over his face, then he came to himself, nodded, smiled, became the Arne she was used to, sat at her table and talked. She heard nothing. She could not answer. He began to look worried, noticing the cold coffee in front of her, brought a glass of water, pleaded with her to explain, until finally she managed to half whisper the things she had seen, the girl, the street, confessing that she had spied on him.

She saw him harden, then go to pieces. Hands covering his face, sobbing like a child, he told her everything. She did not remember how they had managed to get home, but soon the whole street knew about it, for he had insisted on confessing his sins in public in true Salvation Army style. Anne-Marie forgave him, but became curiously quiet. Then one day he left without any warning, gassed both himself and a young lady recruit in a dismal room and left no word whatever. That was the bitter end of Arne. What had happened to Anne-Marie? Listless and still forgiving, she had even attended the funeral and not shed a tear. Then one of their aunts suggested the holiday on the island—long holidays were supposed to help— it seemed a great idea.

It was also something of a shock, that island paradise—grey lichen, carpets of violets, a few gnarled pine-trees, seabirds nesting in their hundreds and the green, ferocious sea at their feet. After taking many buses and boats they ended up there bewildered and totally lost, not knowing what to do. But the house was in working order and the boat would return in two days with provisions. They felt the change, at least Mrs Larsson and Barbro did, but to Anne-Marie it seemed to make no difference, she was as passive as ever and as uncommunicative.

The first week she rested and slept, never dressed, never thought of getting up. Mrs Larsson decided she had made a great mistake and must change her plans, but that somehow wasn't possible—especially since at that very moment Anne-Marie made up her mind, for what reason they never knew, to get out of bed. She faced the sun and got dressed. So they stayed on. But now they had new worries, for Anne-Marie disappeared early before they were awake and returned late in the afternoon. However much they pleaded with her, she would still vanish day after day.

The so-called island actually consisted of three small inter-

connected islets, the one with the house being the largest, with
its small wood; the entire area could be walked over in less than
a couple of hours. And it was as if she didn't want their
company. She started to avoid their eyes. The moment Anne-
Marie was threatened with a possible return to town, she
became more obedient, promised she would stay within call of
them, and thus she had taken over the beach below the house.
All day long she skimmed it for shells, pretty stones, seaweeds,
with which she seemed to communicate, endlessly conversing
with them. Heaps of her salvage were everywhere on the rocks.
She appeared somewhat happier.

They heard her humming to herself and were surprised to be
awoken by a knock on the door and have cups of coffee placed
by their beds. It was as though the old Anne-Marie had come
back to them. She wanted to show them something. On the
verandah a large seagull was standing in a box and, when they
appeared, didn't move away but looked at Anne-Marie. She had
found it separated from the others because of a broken wing,
had fed it daily, and so it had become tame and started to
follow her like a dog.

Though happy about her new interest, they kept the bird at a
distance as it didn't seem to trust anyone but Anne-Marie. It
had a habit of shrieking and flapping its unbroken wing when
they approached. The picture that had disturbed me so much
was taken then, so now I knew why there was a kind of madness in her look, which obviously they hadn't noticed. They
were just so happy about her return to them, the fact that she
talked, did little chores, behaved more normally — so they
decided for her sake and the bird's to stay on another week.
Anne-Marie felt she could cure it, so that it could return to the
flock before they left.

So life was centred on the bird, which stayed with her in the
kitchen all night and was happy with her, it seemed, on the
beach. They made an odd pair.

And then it all changed. The bird would gloomily sit and
stare out to sea, it stopped making angry noises at them,

c

refused to stay indoors and wouldn't take the food offered. Anne-Marie couldn't sleep for worry and kept blaming herself. Nothing they said had any effect. They saw her praying on the rock and crying at the sunset to make the bird better. It started to lose its looks, not bothering to preen itself any more, and then one morning it went into hiding in a thicket. Finally she found it and carried it out into the blazing sun. It was barely alive and made noises suggesting pain. It couldn't use its legs any longer and as she turned it over to examine it more closely a stink so nauseating exuded from it that she was almost sick. Under its broken wing there were hundreds of crawling worms and eggs on a festering sore.

Almost without thinking she took the bird back to the wood-shed by the house, laid it on a chopping block and with one clean blow cut off its head. She buried the twitching body in the sand and kept the head to show them. It took them a long time to get out of her what had happened. She spent hours washing her hands and crying. She couldn't get them clean, she said. And soon she was washing her whole body, her hair, everything had become dirty, and that was how in error she had taken a bottle of peroxide, thinking it was shampoo, and washed her hair with it—and hence the odd straw-coloured effect.

Washing herself, the constant changing of clothes, now became a mania and she stopped talking altogether. And then the pacing started. They left hurriedly; head hanging, eyes downcast, she was as if deaf and dumb, hadn't touched food for a week, couldn't swallow, only whispered, so off she went to the doctors again, who took her to a mental clinic where she deteriorated, it seems. She had to be shut up in a room because of her violence, and shock-treatment followed. That's when she invented her walk—and now all of a sudden it became clear what that last movement of hers meant. It must have sym-bolized the killing of the bird.

She was sent home. There was not much they could do for her now. She was harmless. And her mother and sister had learnt to live with it. It had happened less than two summers ago.

I wonder if Mrs Larsson ever feels guilty about starting to spy on Arne—would Anne-Marie have found out by herself and would she have learnt to live with a lie, as apparently so many women do?

Finally I was released. I was allowed to go home, and I did something which I never normally do, I drew the curtains against the summer sun and tried to sleep, but instead I found myself pacing round the flat aimlessly, unable to concentrate on the Sunday papers or work or watch a TV programme I was supposed to review. And then after giving up all my bad plans about seeing people, going to the cinema, anything, I went to bed and slept as peacefully as a child. And dreamt about you.

In the morning my mind was made up. I was at last ready for you without any hesitations, I didn't know when or how I was going to tell you, but just the knowledge and certainty made everything easy and completely calmed me. What's more, I can't remember ever having been so happy. It was as if through Anne-Marie I had been reborn, able to face myself more honestly. One day it will be very clear to me how it all came to pass. So now when I sit with your telegram in my shaking hand, with tears running down my cheeks of pure, unadulterated happiness, my head spins, my shoddy flat has become a palace into which in a few days you will step. Yes, yes, I'm ready too. And the most marvellous thing is that we made the decision together with miles of oceans and lands and barriers between us.

Two

They put labels on everyone here, they classify us. We are cases of paranoia, schizophrenia and hysteria of multiple personality, which are among the many terms I have heard whispered during my interviews with the high overlords. We are all lumped together in fine-sounding phrases like *dementia praecox*, namely persons of unsound mind, in other words plain mad in the eyes of the hostile world that dares not follow our strange inner wanderings — so they will continue to sing off-key around us while we catch the purest of notes from time to time. Yes, we risk our so-called sanity for the joys of being sometimes truly alive.

Around me here are the maniacs, the senile and feeble-minded, the neurotics. I don't count myself among them; it would make the angels weep to see me in this collective mad-house, though I am not treated quite as the others are. I have more freedom, for I am too valuable a specimen and fit no particular classification. We — you — I — should be given the perfect freedom of being cared for with understanding but otherwise left alone. We should have total liberty within these walls.

It is comfortable enough, with the swimming-pool, the tennis court, the private room and the large wild garden so perfectly suited to our love. The library I quarrel with, for it could be much more extensive; I have asked them so many times for the books you have mentioned, but they will not get them for me. This I find deeply frustrating. I feel how much time I am wasting between our contacts and that makes me unhappy, angry, and my violent self takes over and my spirit, yours, leaves me, which I know is only destructive.

I want them to leave me in peace in order to get on and to soar high, but they cannot ever begin to understand that other kind of seeing which we share. They belong to the hypnotized conformists of the world, so will stay for ever earth-bound. To them the free spirits like ours, one dead, one alive, with centuries between us, are an impossibility. We are madmen let loose. We become dangerous to their securities which, if they dared to examine themselves for a change, would turn out not to exist. They are all too frightened to want to know, yet they meddle and investigate; their inner minds are shut so they get no answers, only total confusion.

It is only when anger fills me that I become really scared. I want revenge for their clumsy interjections, when they hinder me, and sometimes I feel a deep hurt because of my loss of wings. Why shouldn't I be ready for you yet? But then much of the time I do not fear, because as you yourself have said *amor ipse notitia est*. I told them this yesterday, but as their knowledge of Latin is scant I had to translate for them. Love — yes, they got that. But 'is itself a knowing' they found as usual too esoteric to grasp.

Tomorrow I have another session with about six prominent men and it will start from the beginning again, a boring routine. Their fascination with my case makes them greedy for the horse's mouth, as the saying is, and they are full of sly tricks. But never have I changed my story. There is only one that is true. Although I find my time wasted, repeating the past when I want to learn more, I still have to play with them. I have to accept the interrogators in order to gain more freedom later, which they will give if I have collaborated — sweets for the good little girl. They will perform no operation (which I have seen done to others here) because of the uniqueness of my case. They cannot afford to lose their research victim.

So I play with them, eat the meals that are put in front of me, weigh myself on the scales day and night, close my door and turn the lights out at the right time. To all this I conform, only to be left alone with you, to abandon myself and move

beyond — self-transcendence, you said just now. And you also
said that my so-called split mind was perhaps a necessity for
catching a glimpse of heavens which an earth body could never
begin to imagine.

They have many worries about me — my seamy background,
for instance, the lack of almost everything in it. But they cannot
deny my intelligence in spite of all and they are surprised at my
powers of reasoning, that I can offer classifications as good as
theirs. But of course what floors them most is my knowledge
of things which they themselves have left behind in their
various universities. Tomorrow I believe the professor from
Berlin is coming, an expert in ancient Chinese, not only a
Sinologist but also interested in the alchemical scene of the
early period. Well, we shall certainly be able to answer the
questions, whatever they are.

Sometimes, feeling childishly naughty, I am so amused by
their raised eyebrows and open mouths that I start my symbol
writing and, just to confuse them even more, launch into yet
other languages which they know I have never had an earthly
chance of learning. My whole young life was so unsatisfactory
and I can't make them understand my hurry to be reborn with
you, in you, to achieve that hermaphrodite union. There is still
such a lot to learn before I reach the incorruptible breath-body
which grows in the golden flower or in the field of the square
inch, as the text tells us.

Sometimes I call them the death-eaters (they are fascinated by
my vocabulary) because they do really represent the dark masses
who do not challenge new worlds, who take no risks and are
therefore dead. Our consciousness, our search, you say, also
have their risks. They also make us sometimes melancholy and
lonely — we do get the blue devils, don't we? — and we become
impatient, even despairing, and we do from time to time go
mad. Yes, but we accept the risks, we are not like them, we
are not dead. Nor will we ever die.

I cannot reach you with a new soul language, but I want to

invent a sensual language of the body that would make your heart melt. You have forgotten what the body was really like and you said that you also wanted to share with me those sensations. You said that once you used to let yourself sink into the high grasses and try to become one with the earth beneath. Your head would begin to swim and you lost yourself completely in it. But that was so long ago.

I have knocked on the door of the mysteries of nature and have been granted entry, so now I can see into the lowest earthly depths and also into the deepest hell, which leads me in a roundabout way into a third heaven. I no longer need my spy-glass to dissect. My eyes have gained a new power and I see details that upset my body to the point of vomiting. I have reached the point where I can see the fluids and the power moving through the delicate pale stalks of a plant, the whole system of circulation, and I can almost penetrate the growing flower to its very root. I see and hear its actual mode of breathing; its scent-calls to bees and other insects become vivid and clear. The yellow petals of some flowers look in the sun like gold thinned out under the alchemist's hammer; and the pollen turns into worlds of golden globules, each intricately carved and decorated. And every single one of the most miniscule worlds that open up for me is totally different.

How can I give all this to you? You talked to me some time ago about the two-fold seeing and hearing, an inward and an outward, so that we should be able to judge spiritual things with the inward part, the deity concealed in matter, the heavenly, *deus absconditus*. But because I am so feeble, so far from the innermost, I can only use all the puny words in the dictionary.

Where is my new language? I despair because I can't get the words to flow like the water in the brook. Only in the fashion of a travelogue can I describe to you the sanatorium, its beautiful isolated garden, the moss fountain that drips mysteriously on to slippery rocks, the exotic flowers, the palm trees. I was so lucky to be sent to a place where long ago a botanist had been at work, allowed to indulge his every taste.

But then that is just as it should be—we have a right to an earthly paradise, nothing else is good enough for us. Just let everyone keep us happy and protect our solitude, for me to reach closer and get your second sight, to find the hidden letters, the sealed books, the secrets, and for me to extract wisdom from that stupid self.

They interrogate me with such disbelief in their eyes, but also with a certain amount of panic. I can see their excitement. They are supposed to be knowledgeable and wise and they are seven against me. They thumb through my files with sombre faces. The papers are dog-eared from all the work they have already done at home and they are none the wiser for it; if anything, it has only confused them more.

Again, my physical health is another factor against my 'split' mind. Only my fits of anger make them sit up in hope, to be disappointed when I emerge at the other end just as clean and conscious of who I am and what I am doing. Nevertheless, they somehow feel they can diagnose my madness in those fits. My non-existent childhood lies in front of them, black little words strung together and meaning nothing—that I stopped school at the age of twelve after a sudden coma and all my past vanished in a single moment. Nothing was ever the same again, how could it have been?

However, it all makes nonsense of any possibility of my knowledge, my Latin texts and alchemy and you, Paracelsus. They can never understand the transformation, how first I took the place of your mother whom you had lost and loved so deeply, through to the time when I became the sister, the close one, until finally I was the beloved, for whom you chose the name Melusina, since she arises in the imagination and inhabits the blood and was born in the womb of mysteries. Thus I too came into the world and centuries will pass before our love is completed.

That you were a healer and magician and alchemist you have proved again and again to them, but they are fools who want to test things under microscopes and take samples in test-tubes, in which they will find nothing but emptiness and dust. They have no power over me, us, except in their needles and they know it, so I rattle off my answers to them. When for instance I tell them that the task of alchemy is like shooting an arrow through a thread hung up in the clouds they just laugh, but note it down all the same somewhat uneasily.

Meanwhile, my hand goes on writing in a large Latin script. 'Man must be regarded as a small world, for he is like a world in every way. The bones beneath the skin must be compared to the mountains, for they strengthen the body just as rocks strengthen the earth, and the flesh compares with the earth itself and the arteries become the rivers and the blood vessels the streams that empty into the rivers. And both small and large waters pour down into the sea, which is the bladder. Between sprouting hair and growing herbs there is also this link, and all else that lives within a man or outside him, whatever it may be, is likened to its counterpart in the world.'

I translate; and point out that it is an old alchemical text, not me, and that you have just given me this message. They write down my translation solemnly and add the text to their files and ask when you lived — from 1493 to 1541, they know the answer as well as I do. They have looked you up in their reference books and found me correct.

The room is becoming dim and I can almost see your aura that holds me so powerfully. You practically shout to me now as the light, your light, begins to warm me — 'With your own flame you must burn yourself to ashes, for how otherwise can you expect to become new?' I cannot convince them of anything; from far away I hear their explanations, internal hearing, pathological schizoid, extra-sensory perception, words, words that mean nothing to me. I try feebly to impress upon them, however, that I do not suffer from delusional thinking, but that they do, because they only know one world and I have at least two. Haven't I given them proof after proof? What about your letters? Ah, they say, you wrote them to yourself, dear. And what about the messages, the language? In any case it wasn't at all my way of writing. Automatic—again I hear them argue.

I'm tired now. I can feel myself gliding away and I can only hear you coming very strongly. 'Only when a certain awareness and sensitivity have been achieved can a person stop living with only a small part of himself.' The room has become at least ten times as light, lighter than anything I have seen with my outer eyes. It fills the entire place and seems to have an immense depth—and no centre. I'm being put on a stretcher and I can smell the injection they are preparing. They have to hold me down, I don't know how many of them—and I become wild and strong in my despair, I scream and scream, I want to vomit blood from the depths of me, since blood is the primitive symbol for the soul and they want to kill it, and I hear myself cry in panic before I'm out and all goes black, 'What is this life you want me to live?' But I get no answer from either them or you.

The sharp sun lit the open book as it lay among files and hypodermic needles, the dust vibrating over the large script and never falling on the words, the sentences. The medical professors with their withered laurels frowned upon the book that made them feel as insecure as little boys. Almost with averted eyes they read: 'Psychic facts of serious import are not susceptive to weights and measures, microscopes or test-tubes. People thus suppose them beyond determination, but it is only that they are the exclusive property of those who know them inwardly, just as it is useless to display bright colours to a blind man.'

'One in the eye for us, I suppose,' said the hospital psychiatrist, looking even more hysterical than usual. He was constantly drumming his chubby fingers on table-tops and his feet beat an odd rhythm against the stone floor. He was unaware of his nervous habits and the irritation they caused. With hostile thoughts in all their minds they still could not leave the book alone. 'If a bad man uses good means, the good means function in a bad way … ' The script appeared to be in the meticulous hand of a holy man who had spent his days in solitude doing nothing else but writing. They saw all this and were dumbfounded by it. She herself had said a few minutes earlier, 'I don't write like that.'

'In man only faith is capable of working miracles … In all that is in nature the outward eye can never perceive the truth; only the mind can. This truth contains the art of liberating the spirit; concealed within it lies the philosopher's stone.'

'What bubbles Mr Superman blows,' the psychiatrist said. The German expert kept clearing his throat; and he cleaned his monocle carefully and said nothing.

'Light springs from darkness, things unconscious burst into the conscious, man follows the star of imagination.'

'More and more nebulosity,' muttered someone. The professor stared out of the window with weary eyes, seeing the sky change to a deeper purple, hearing a distant murmur.

'Bea then covered Gabricus and drew him into her womb, so that he was no longer visible. And she enclosed Gabricus in so much love that he became utterly a part of herself, and separated him into inseparable parts.'

'What a delightful family — and I assume they lived happily ever after.' The obstetrician could contain himself no longer. 'What utter nonsense.'

At last the professor put his monocle back, stared hard at the page and said in a taut voice, as if to himself, 'And you say that this girl has never had access to such literature?'

'None. She is almost illiterate,' said the house doctor. He was firm in voice despite the soft sensual mouth, the weak chin, the flabby body, and he was perspiring despite the fan above his head.

'And you say she is virgo intacta?'

The psychiatrist drummed more loudly with his feet. 'Oh, she has totally surrendered to this phantom and taken the veil for him, as it were. He's the Mr Big in her life.'

The house doctor handed over a physical report. 'She's in good order. She leads a life of self-denial, almost monastic. We can't get her to join in any of the activities here. And she has no relationship with any of us — treats us as if we didn't exist.'

'I offer you such insight that you will be able to see things concealed in the shadow. But the way is perilous. All good things have their price and to develop the self is one of the most expensive of good things … ' Then suddenly *'life intensified'* was written on a page by itself accompanied by a drawing of a mandala with golden flowers and a sun around it.

The professor frowned and stood up and paced the room in a schoolmasterly fashion. 'This whole matter has to be investigated more seriously,' he said. 'There must be some kind of fraud involved and, if so, it is very clever indeed, the work of an expert.' And he looked suspiciously at the assembly of so-called experts, the investigators.

'You're not suggesting that anyone here is concerned?' The house doctor was offended; he blushed. 'The case has been most closely studied by all of us here. It is being handled with care, as the situation is delicate — we certainly don't want the news to leak out and have queues of journalists and television cameras turning a private institution into a public laughing-stock.'

'Yes,' said the psychiatrist eagerly. 'Are you actually saying that you believe in a lunatic you have in your care? Very fine publicity, I must say.'

'Exactly,' said the professor with a sardonic smile. 'That's just what you're doing with this report, don't you see? You are believing it, when the entire thing is a plot to fool you. I find it monstrous, which is why I propose an investigation in every sense of the word. I wouldn't even worry about bringing the police into it.'

'How very German,' murmured the young doctor.

'I beg your pardon?' said the professor.

'But the nurse has seen her writing this script. We have seen her writing it today in front of us all,' the house doctor said nervously. 'And in any case, what about her spoken words?'

'Anything can be taught by someone very clever — cleverer

than you have been, I fear.' His tone was poisonous. 'I cannot believe it comes from this girl, from this disturbed mind – the sentences are too clear, too symbolic, too true, there is too much wisdom, too much knowledge. The Syrian, the Chinese are there, as well as the later Byzantine. As you know, I'm not inexpert in these fields, and it's quite plain to me that the person involved is most knowledgeable.'

There was a hush in the room. The house doctor was silenced for the moment. Monocle once more in place, the professor read aloud in a severe tone: 'Concealed in you are treasures which you must explore. Anyone who richly develops the inner parts of himself will see the proper brilliance of the yellow light.' He paused. 'You see, gentlemen, that's a typical example. La-chang wu, from an ancient Chinese treatise on alchemy.' The professor, growing indignant, read on none the less, his hands shaking slightly. The room was tense. It had become uncannily dark. A light was switched on. The words seemed to vibrate. 'Heaven is man, man heaven, all men being one heaven, heaven being only one man. To generate itself is the most natural and perfect thing a creature can do ... Paracelsus,' the professor declared. He was perspiring slightly. 'We shall perform a supreme act of the body with the pure chemistry of the spirit, with the true gold, the wise stone – that is just what the saints have managed time and time again. You will be called mad, but everything beyond the limits of the mind is condemned by that same mind as lunatic.'

'Hear, hear,' said the house doctor under his breath.

'But it is only termed madness because of ignorance – and men are now ignorant. There is a heavenly light that man cannot absorb from outside; it can only come from within. That light was discovered by Abel, it was in Solomon's heart, the miracles of Moses, of the prophets, sprang from that light. Elias survived in the desert by means of it and thus Christ fasted for forty days. It enabled Moses to build the tabernacle, Noah the ark, Solomon the temple.' He paused. 'Mr Superman really seems to know his stuff.'

The psychiatrist scratched the eczema on his right knee. His hands were clammy.

'To flash a few seconds of the truth upon the world would be to change it so that life might begin again.'

A sudden thunder-clap surprised them. They had hardly noticed that the storm had moved fast and was now above them, cutting through the sky, blinding the room for a second. All the lights fused, electric wires sizzled, then another horrendous thunder-clap was followed by a crash outside in the garden. Like a horde of frightened animals they ran to the window, staring out in disbelief at the ancient oak in the middle of the court, which was in flames. Only the house doctor continued sitting in his chair, with a hand on his heart. He looked agitated and was breathing with difficulty. The rain, sweeping over the court, smattered like angry words and soon turned to hail. The tree was a black smoking ruin, the ground was flooded. It was like the beginning and the end. No one had anything to say.

Sister Ann, who was on night duty, tiptoed round the sick room and at last tucked the blankets gently in over the body. It was a perfectly made bed, not a wrinkle to be seen, and she was secretly proud of it. But she was glad to leave the room—she felt ill at ease and did not quite know why, perhaps because she really liked the woman and was sorry for what they had to do to her in these violent fits. As she softly closed the door, the laughter broke out and her heart almost stopped before she fled in panic to her cubbyhole, where she switched on the radio so as not to hear.

It was a commanding laugh that seemed to have nothing to do with the frail body that lay cramped in the strait-jacket in the bare cold room of the special ward. From deep caverns it welled up and, once out, it appeared to fill every bit of space around the laughing woman, the vibrations tickled her toes, her head was a swirling, tolling bell, the whole electric-chemical network of consciousness was swinging. It was uncontrollable and it

D

shocked the room, even the bed seemed to want to answer back as it squeaked under her.

It was a laugh so monstrous and catching that the young night-nurse found herself stopping in the corridor and giggling hysterically before hurrying to answer an important bell. It was insane—or was she? She could no longer think; the laugh reverberated in her head.

On the ceiling of the sick room a comedy was in full performance. She had her eyes wide open. Soldiers and statesmen, diplomats and flea-trainers, clerics and jay-walkers and millions of people of every race, businessmen and Jacks of all trades trotted after one another splitting their sides. They had been granted a revelation: 'the world is insane', they hollered to one another, unable quite to believe it and slapping one another's backs. She saw institutions crumble, foundations give way, law and order surrender their precarious hold, police officers cry in their handkerchiefs with joy. The sky above them was full of fingerprints, prison keys, inkwells and rubber stamps, handcuffs, barbed wire, watch dogs, barriers. All suspicion floated away on a cloud of laughter. Accountants and tax-officers screamed their heads off and made a ring of roses round a pile of forms, receipts, ledgers, balance-sheets, until it all exploded and became a magnificent aurora borealis which lit and warmed the earth after the sun's disappearance. Churches, chapels, synagogues, curled up like sleepy dogs in front of it. Cloisters, crucifixes, cardinals' hats, the papal ring, were ripped, broken, crushed, and their owners forced to join the laughing queue which had formed to celebrate the big joke of the world, and so it came to pass that blacks and whites, archbishops, pimps, Jesuits, mothers superior, whores and missionaries held hands and laughed and laughed while the choirboys sang side-bursting hymns that made nonsense of the holy weeks and all the masses, and libraries tore their own pages in ecstasy, rolled over each other like so many clowns and cried with laughter at their pompous insides.

The laughter so tightly filled the room that it had to squeeze out through the keyhole and, once free, nothing could stop it. It galloped down the gleaming corridor that had never heard anything like it, it pressed itself through narrow chinks in the windows to deliver its message that the world had finally accepted its own raving madness, it astounded the paving-stones, rattled the cobbles and made the grasses bend double as if in pain. The laugh shouted for love, expansion of awareness, change, illumination, joy and again love, which included all possible freedoms, brotherhoods, the banishment of injustice. Neither shouting nor laughing could stop or be stopped, and all of a sudden it seemed possible that the world could change. On her rounds the little night-sister heard the laughter all the time and now had turned to a pillar of stone outside the chamber.

For what seemed a brief second she took its message and laughed aloud, though she had never considered life a laughing matter. She saw her puny little wonderings as if for the first time, as if they were all happening in space. She struggled vainly against the laughter welling up inside her, and soon small trickles of tears ran down her plump and otherwise un-troubled cheeks, and her laughter was filled with pain. She saw this tiny and neatly labelled parcel called Sister Ann surrounded by swirling rubber gloves, syringes, bed-pans, gauzes and slops; and the little parcel that was herself making beds for eternity, folding, tucking in, smoothing, folding, tucking in, *ad infinitum*. She broke down and sobbed now, yet she could not stop laughing at all the thousands of beds waiting to be made and tucked in. She fled with the laughter pursuing her, prancing, side-stepping, clowning, until she dissolved in hysterics.

The night was still black with not the slightest hope of dawn. Other patients had woken. There was a ringing of bells, a clamour of voices, bangs on the wall, screams of pain. Ann fell into the head nurse's arms and had no explanation to offer, only sobs amid the subsiding laughter. Firmly the head nurse took over. Hands went out for syringe, cotton wool, the needle sucking up the syrupy substance from a neatly labelled bottle.

Her clacking heels reverberated in the corridor for everyone to note—yes, even the laughter, which paused and took breath. The firm steps sprang from years of loneliness which had made for a certain bitter immunity, and these steps shouted no to the laughter, death to its voice of love and freedom, and she shut her ears to enchantment and change, she trampled on the compassions—until finally the laughter stopped. For a moment it had had the upper destructive hand.

As she walked back, the corridor had become quieter than ever, as cold and quiet as only the grave could be, and much against her will she caught herself thinking of her own life, that fenced-in life of hers, the secrets she tried to keep even from herself, her miserable marriage, her hatred of almost everything, all those clothes in closets which forever needed spring-cleaning, the tables, the chairs, the whole dusty flat lying lifeless in front of her.

The night fell asleep, but little Sister Ann was still crying softly in her cubbyhole that smelt of sour coffee and stale bread. The head nurse put a tranquilliser in her hand. She was still cross and showed it. She was also tired and overworked and middle-aged and looked it. She sat lumpishly in the chair, curbing the desire to cry. She pretended to fall asleep but was increasingly awake.

The square box of the cell stood grey and cold in the steely morning light. The windows were darkened ponds that mirrored the bed, the basin and the chair. The blue night-light, gleaming over her like a halo, gave the face an unworldly shine.

It now seemed impossible that the once so clownish laughter could have welled out of that mouth or had a seat in that frail body. Her face was still slightly twisted, mouth curling upwards, perhaps waiting to start its strange wanderings once more. Her skin, now tightly drawn over the bones, was unwrinkled. Her eyes were firmly shut; only the eyebrows showed a faint surprise, as if questioning herself or something else.

The air was still, as in a silent tomb. This was not a sleep as the sleeper knew it. For a while she had been put out of action against her will, but life held its breath for her while the body on the bed was biding its time.

And her inner eye saw the words in the clouds written in gold. My lonely creature, you are finding the path to yourself. And your past goes beyond yourself and the seven devils that are in you.

Three

The one place for hiding the crumbling face and the inevitable tears on a Sunday morning was the bathroom. He always locked himself in for the customary cry while at the same time trying to keep busy, either cleaning the washbasin that still smelt faintly of sick or scrubbing the bath that somebody had always left smeared. To pretend that the tears weren't there wasn't easy; they fell too saltily on the lips.

They laughed at his exaggerated prissiness and why not, let them laugh, why not, let them tease what didn't really matter. He had to admit that he was obsessed by cleaning, polishing, dusting, scrubbing things. It gave him the greatest satisfaction to lay his hand on shiny surfaces. With the toilet-roll replenished, the plastic box of Kleenex refilled, the clean towels hanging white and frothy over the aluminium rail with not a fingerprint to be seen on it, he felt slightly fulfilled and somehow more real. Trying to avoid himself in the mirror while washing was a bit hard; when he started shaving his pale stubbly growth, it became impossible.

He wasn't a bad addition to the seedy monkey-world he had chosen to be involved in, the world that was slowly making itself heard in the room next door. He pulled faces at himself which made him even more inhuman and tried desperately to avoid the frightened eyes, the sensual mouth that didn't seem to belong to the face that emerged out of the lather. The proper old-fashioned shave had its appeal; it became a ritual and took time, which was always something to be killed.

The group met after work on the Saturday afternoon and usually chose his flat as the most convenient. There were four of them including himself. They had gone on for over two years now, and if anyone dared to be truly honest they remained together only for companionship, a certain feeling of familiarity.

Now the little zoo in miniature was waking up in earnest and growing noisy. There were a few loud shrieks. He presumed they must be bitching about sex, the favourite topic, everyone pretending to be madly sexy but always with more talk than action.

He certainly didn't find himself desirable when he caught another glimpse in the misted-up mirror. As for anyone else seeing anything in that skimpy body with the beginnings of a pot and the pathetic foreskin hanging limply between his legs, well, the idea was beyond him. But the legs weren't bad, in fact quite pretty; he admired them slyly.

And now they were rapping on the door and shouting for breakfast, so he would have to hurry up. A smell of fresh coffee penetrated the bathroom and he thought of home, of Mother and of Sunday dinner. She would have prepared all his favourite dishes of course, she adored spoiling him and he would have felt so good, even talented, because there would be talk of his promotion in the shop, and he would give her the latest of his home-made pendants — no good telling her that after a certain time in his job more responsibility and a better salary were unavoidable unless you were a total imbecile, and pointless to say that he was about the worst in the jewellery class. He was already an artist in her eyes, so he kept it up as much for her sake as for anything else, though he knew he would never improve even if he tried harder or liked it more.

Anyway, because of this jewellery, he was always called upon to add the artistic touches to table decorations and flower arrangements, and strangely enough nobody commented on the messes he made of colour combinations or the way the vases nearly toppled over. And the same with his cooking — it was supposed to be so inventive and casual, yet however much he garnished everything with fancy-cut tomatoes and frilly parsley, underneath he felt it was bland, grey, reminiscent of dog food.

The only cooking he did well was sweet things, puddings and cakes, but then he had learnt that from her. They used to have such fun in the kitchen. He thought of the sweet cake-mix in the bowl that he was allowed to lick clean and could almost smell the vanilla and the grated lemon.

He buried his face in the soft towel and had another little outburst of tears.

The world outside the window hardly looked welcoming or friendly: the car-parks on his doorstep with every place filled, criss-cross roads, a few dismal trees, several playgrounds, drawing-board ideas come true, a cement world for people like him to sit and have sick reflections in. Some children bundled up against the cold were making snow-angels, throwing themselves flat on the snow with shouts of joy, flapping their arms to and fro, making wings. Why had he never played those games, why had he always been so frightened of other children, and why had he only been happy around her skirts and in her kitchen? He thought of her and felt lost. Once he had believed some magic thing would happen to him. He had never forgotten the stories they read together, toads turning into princes at the touch of a wand.

Now, almost middle-aged, he surely ought to give up childish ideas of a miracle and just accept himself. But it was hard to admit that he was a failure, and of course his friends were all the same, tedious little shop assistants or waiters, sailors, train attendants. He knew he was firmly stuck in the grey middle brigade. He sank his face into the icy cold water in the washbasin and held his breath for as long as he could stand it, it seemed an age, and came out panting, eyes bloodshot, slightly dizzy. Silly fool, having little games with death, but he felt the better for it.

He powdered his face white and applied some mascara—at least he could look extraordinary—and combed the long lank hair round a black velvet ribbon. Then the white tights and ballet shoes and the big-flowered shirt with the wide sleeves made the transfiguration complete.

Someone had put on a record and the music was crude and loud. He liked the music of Strauss and shared Mother's taste for the old Lehár operettas, but there was no point in admitting it to the boys. They would only scream him down and call him hopelessly old-fashioned. In any case he kept personal things like the family away from them, even removing, before he left for work on Saturday morning, the photos that were all over the flat.

He had once discovered them gloating over his dear familiar faces in their gilt frames. They had especially roared at the wedding picture, finding the combination hilarious: Dad tight-faced and weedy like himself—'What could she have seen in him?' He had never noticed Dad's ugliness with such clarity, or how deeply unsuitable a pair they were—because his Mother, though enormous and buxom, at least looked healthy and even quite pretty. Anyway, he felt safer with their faces hidden in his desk, safer too because she couldn't see what he was up to.

Irritated with him now, they banged even more loudly on the door. It was finally Olle who shouted, 'If you want a pile on the carpet it's all right with me—only hope you've got some strong detergent.' They all laughed behind the shut door; someone blew a whistling fart and they became hysterical with giggling, so he hurriedly put the silver cross in his one pierced ear, dangled it in a wicked manner, bared his teeth, fluttered the eyelashes and stepped out.

'So that's what our beauty has been doing,' Hasse cackled like a broody hen. 'Come on, turn round and show us your lovely masterpiece.' He was sitting swaddled in bedclothes on the sofa, still having his breakfast. Nils looked at the crumbs of cornflakes and bread, the spilt coffee on the sheets, and frowned. Hasse said, 'Oh Beauty, come on now, you can't be cross with Mum, she'll tidy it up in her own time ... '

'Where did you get that shirt, fell off a lorry, did it?' Olle said, slinking into the bathroom without waiting for a reply.

'Oh, but it's lovely, it really is,' Hasse said, sensing his disappointment. 'It all is lovely, very unusual, it reminds me of my days in the chorus, oh my dear boy, what a choice we had, every single one of them a poof ... ' His eyes rolled to heaven and he almost broke into song with excitement.

Nils could see the reminiscences coming up fast; they must not be encouraged or he would have all the old tatty stories for the umpteenth time. He dusted the surfaces with his hand as he walked to the kitchen for a cold cup of coffee. Hasse droned on in the other room while he made himself an enormous sand-wich of hard rye-bread with the left-overs from last night, and he felt unwanted, unloved and as gloomy as the grey outside. The crunching of his jaws kept Hasse's monologue at a distance, but he could hear the excited shriek from time to time while swallowing and caught the occasional word, Carmen, tights, dressing-rooms, even chickens. A jazzy number burst out; Olle was back from the bathroom, shouting, 'Come on Beauty, don't sulk, do your routine and cheer the old lady up, she's in tears over her lost youth.'

He did his curious pantomime in a deadpan manner, a bit of ballet, a 'thirties tap, with something of his own now and then thrown in, odd little flaps, tiptoeing, the swirls of a dervish. He saw himself as though from above and, aware of the ridiculous figure he was cutting, started burlesquing it even more to get the laughs, wiggling his bottom flirtatiously at Hasse. He hated the effeminate act he was putting on, yet couldn't stop it, he tried to work himself up to stop the brain functioning, he wanted to become the total fool, the clown—he would have to return soon enough to the grey.

Physically they were a crude bunch in comparison to him, he thought, circling round them, almost tripping over Olle's legs. Olle was sitting on the floor sorting out records, dressed only in his grubby underpants and wriggling gracelessly. He was on the drapery counter, and was pretty in a butch way and always the one to keep them entertained with gossip, his begin-ning and end.

Hasse was mother to them all. He had been a waiter at the Central Hotel for almost twenty years and lived in a room there

with two budgerigars and a pair of bored goldfish endlessly
circling in a bowl. Always the noisy one, he had to be hushed
down in the street—too easily over-excited, with an embarrassingly high-pitched laugh. Nils always tried to avoid being
with him in public places; it was all too obvious what kind of
partner he was. But Hasse was a good-natured soul and showed
a soft heart for people in need or distress.

They had met at the Hotel, where meaningful glances had
passed over the steak and onions which Hasse served him.

A bell rang. He danced across to the door and looked
through the peep-hole. Yes, it was Tage all right, on time,
dressed in his usual ridiculous garb, the old weatherbeaten
lumber-jacket, ski-boots, the Austrian hat with the brush, and a
rather slack rucksack on his shoulders, the complete sportsman.
He was supposed to be out for a long country walk to lose
weight; there was a thermos and a pack of sandwiches lovingly
cut and buttered by his wife or one of his three devoted
daughters.

He danced round Tage while helping him off with the
camouflage and putting a frilly apron over the elephantine
trousers which Tage insisted on wearing. He looked like an old
matron sitting in the big chair which he had somehow reserved
for himself and he was soon busy on the embroidery which he
kept in the flat. He had taken over his father's locksmith
business; he was a respected townsman. He loved his locks,
bolts, wife, home and daughters. But he was also frightened of
thieves and of being found out, scared stiff of his female world,
doing everything in his power to get away from home. A
member of the council, he had once almost been elected mayor;
he belonged to the Angling Club, a society for amateur photographers, the Magic Circle. Generous in every way, simple-
minded perhaps, he had discovered boys in his fifties and
couldn't get over it, though keener on observing than taking
part.

What a dreary bunch they were, Nils thought while laying
the table. Yet he would rather have them there than be alone

Hasse, dishing up the cold delicacies and doing his motherly duties, scolded and fussed over everyone and everything. Olle was eating tiny sausages in a suggestive manner. Nils consumed more than anyone else; he never seemed to get enough food, spreading the butter an inch thick, piling cheese and radishes and tomatoes on top. He heaped so much potato salad on his plate that there was hardly any room for the ham and sausages and sardines.

The talk during lunch was always childish, but because they quibbled about the most unimportant things it was strangely comforting. He knew almost always what the boys were going to say—or do for that matter. Afterwards Tage brought out from his voluminous trousers the latest 8mm movie and Olle commented crudely as they watched it running backwards; they sometimes found it sexier that way. And Olle brought out the much-thumbed magazines. Always the same— no surprises.

The afternoon somehow ebbed away. As the clock struck the hours in the flat next door with boring regularity someone always fell asleep. Olle did the crossword. Nils made a cake and they had it hot with the butter melting. Hasse watched television. Tage was yawningly at the embroidery again. The day changed from light grey to a leaden darkness; and at about five, as always, Tage looked at his watch and said, 'I'm for home.' Outside it was pitch black.

When they had all left, Nils felt that they had never been there. They left no trace. He changed back into normal clothes and washed off the make-up before he put the family photos in their proper places.

Then he went to the kiosk which stood on a windy corner like an outpost in the wilderness. The woman was reluctant to open her glass shutter; she was snug in her box. A sweet hot air which carried a mixture of bananas, apples and chocolate struck him. It was almost nauseating. Even so he bought a bar with nuts in it and the Sunday paper.

He gobbled the chocolate on the pavement as though in a

hurry. His toes were numb with cold. Then he went back into the queue of pasty-faced, serious gentlemen that had formed. He still felt deprived of something, so bought some more sweets, thinking it might help. While skimming through the paper, he ate the chocolates and the jellies and felt quite sick, but hungry all the same. There was nothing appetizing left on the shelves, but he had a desperate need to chew.

In the end he found a forgotten tin of fish-cakes in white sauce which he heated and consumed with some stale beer and hard bread covered with mayonnaise out of a tube. The butter had run out. It was a dismal meal; yet it all went down; he felt bloated. He then had a bath and watched programme after programme on television without really taking anything in.

He was clean, well-combed and proper again in his pyjamas and dressing-gown when he made the call home.

Yes, of course they had all been up to her place on the Saturday as he could have guessed, Svea and the children and her husband and the dog. They were all well, but Svea was a bit tired these days as she was doing extra work in the sweet-shop. Then the children had been specially tiresome and demanding, what with earaches and infections of one sort and another. Yes, Father was fine but didn't get on very well with the new foreman at the factory. She had a big washing week coming up and had been mending sheets for Svea and herself for days; it was amazing how much you had to pay for poor quality stuff. Every few minutes she worried about the cost of the call to him, but he insisted as usual on the full half-hour. He must send his socks this week and what about the suit that needed a new lining? The old warmth crept up his spine with the familiar voice, he was feeling vaguely happy and it was hard ringing off. As he heard the click at the other end, he still held on. Perhaps she was still there or would come back, had never really left him.

Not to think now, and certainly not to brood, but to keep busy. He dusted the furniture, sprayed the wax at the exact distance from surfaces and polished until he perspired. The air smelt clean and untouched again. This was the smell he preferred to the most expensive perfume, the most exotic incense. The miniature collection of farm animals and the zoo were wiped clean and put into order. He washed his socks, rinsed out his shirt, cleaned his shoes and laid out everything neatly for the morning. He was ready to drop.

While the electric toothbrush was whizzing in his mouth, he thought of all the arrangements for the next day. The sales were starting and he must not forget to put his name on the blankets he wanted for Mother and the overnight suitcase he fancied for himself—he would place his initials on it in gold leaf and it would look smart. And then there was the evening dress, of course, on which he might be rash enough to spend some money for Lola's Saturday party. And perhaps breakfast at the milk-bar as a treat, since he was running short of food. His head was still full of plans when he dozed off, then fell into a sleep with a host of fragmented dreams, of which not one would he remember.

He woke five minutes before the alarm sounded. The moon behind the blinds gave an eerie light, then flooded into the room. He lay blinking at it, without understanding.

He yawned through his dressing and had a foul taste of fish, mayonnaise, chocolates, in his mouth. He brushed his teeth ferociously and did a lot of noisy gargling, while staring down at the bent black figures scraping the ice off windscreens, seeing their breath in the lamplight, chilled by just the thought of going outside.

The lifts had decided to take a day off. He felt a headache mounting as he walked down his seven floors, deciding against the milk-bar even if the pretty boy was behind the counter. Just to order a cup of tea would be too much.

The snow was piled high everywhere. Cars were swaying dangerously on the glistening road. He was almost the only pedestrian in the street, which was a comfort: no need to communicate. The drivers had their windows firmly closed against the frozen air that bit into his nose and cheeks and made them sting and feel curiously alive.

The old hags were already queueing outside the shop and he felt at once a tremendous rage, almost a hatred of them, their faces so vacant, grey, well-fed, so ludicrously behatted, and he loathed himself too, for having to be polite and to bow and to listen to their twaddle. He could not stand the greedy eyes that devoured his goods or all the fingering, and at the same time he hated his own greed in taking advantage of the sale.

He was relieved to be in his department before anyone else. He needed time. He had some chocolate in a paper-cup from the machine; at least it was hot and sweet and somewhat comforting. He did his books, sitting on the radiator. It was still dark outside, it had clouded over and snow was falling and it looked pretty enough now in the lamplight but would probably turn to brown slush by the time he went home again.

The day lay like an abyss in front of him. He could not make up his mind which he disliked most, a slack, dull Monday when everyone was shadowy or a lively day like this with too much edginess and bad temper. The only relief was the lunch-hour, which passed quickly enough. He and Olle took their express-tray at the co-op restaurant and ran through their customers; there was some fun in tearing dutiful citizens to shreds.

But the afternoon was worse. He looked at his watch, never quite understanding time, how the minutes could drag so. Every so often he took a cup of tea or chocolate from the machine. The liquids it produced had a curious sameness and he was furious with himself for spending good money on it but always succumbed. At one moment he rushed out to buy a few odds and ends for his supper and on the way back stood in awe for a few seconds in front of the flower shop and realized that he would not be able to afford flowers again until spring. Then later he collected the weekly money for the holiday club, which had been his bright idea and gave the staff something to look forward to, those fourteen days in Las Palmas where they might meet one another on some promenade.

And finally closing-time and a pitch-black sky again. The same cars were on their way home, windows still closed and steamed up. Men scratched heads and picked noses at traffic-lights. It was cold standing in the queue at the kiosk, his feet ached, noisy gang boys with motor-bikes were buying sausages, everything seemed to be steaming and hissing, yellows and reds from the mustard and ketchup were running over the long naked sausages on to the bread and wrapping. They took their time, ordering mashed potato puffed and creamy in little cartons with wooden spoons, heaping the acid green relish on top. He decided to have some too, never mind the blood pudding and jam he had bought for supper. He bought a couple of beers, the evening paper and the usual sweets, a packet of mentholated cigarettes. He would try to make a cosy evening for himself with television, but he would call Hasse too, which could last as long as an hour if you kept on encouraging him.

He ate the sausages plain with the mashed potato and he ate standing up, while fingering her letter which had arrived that afternoon. It was nice to be able to rely on its waiting there for him. As usual the letter was filled with chit-chat, safe things that could never hurt him, everyday securities. He sat down devouring it while dipping sweet biscuits in some weak tea, feeling at one with her, totally understanding all her problems, the sewing-machine, the new dress that did not quite fit, the knitting she had started, the plants, the prices of things. He read it twice and felt vaguely comforted.

Her eyes grew moist and soft as she thought of him. She had to admit she was a sloppy, sentimental old thing standing there, clutching his letter which had arrived that very Friday morning. He was as fastidious and punctual, as much a creature of habit as she herself. He would never let her down; that security made everything seem rosy, and a warmth spread through her whole body. When she had done the shopping she would read the letter again in their favourite coffee-shop.

She was standing at the butcher's holding her numbered

queue-ticket like a schoolgirl. She never minded waiting. On the contrary, it was a nice time for day-dreams, eyeing the carcases hanging in neat rows on large iron hooks. Everything in the shop looked appetizing—the window with the well-arranged cuts of meat divided by the vivid green plastic parsley, the soft shining white sausages curling round each other in snake-like fashion, the mouth-watering effect of the lighting on the goods. The minced meat heaped into pyramids made her look forward to the meatballs she was going to roll—hundreds of them—and at the same time she would have an equal number of lovely memories to fondle while squeezing the meat into the proper shape.

Nils had always said that they smelt of Saturday, the smell of freedom, holidays, home, and he would have stood beside her rolling them in his dainty hands and regaling her. He had had such grand ideas about the future, she couldn't help smiling to herself: the castles, the limousines, the golden thrones he was going to give her.

She didn't hear her number being called out until someone poked her in the ribs and pointed at her ticket. She was still somewhat dazed when, with the smile lingering on her face, she insisted on a special cut from the carcase which she had earlier selected with her eye.

The assistant tried to persuade her that the cut on the counter—or for that matter the already minced article—was in fact the best they had, but she wouldn't listen to any of that. She liked it to be special for her and also to see the sharp knife go through the enormous untouched beast. And then it had to be minced at least twice to arrive at the texture she wanted. It came wriggling out of the machine, red and raw, in slinky waves on to the waxed paper. She saw them all in her mind's eye, Svea and the children, Tor, and Dad, heard them smack their lips with pleasure, saw them loosening their belts. She always overfed them, but since they never seemed to mind she carried on buying. The assistants looked like busy doctors in surgery walking to and fro—spotlessly white, which was impressive. She would never go to a butcher with bloody or even smeared aprons. The thought was offensive.

The liver-paste was cut almost noiselessly from a large square chunk lying on a glistening white porcelain plate. And how could she resist the galantine that stood in front of her, the jelly shivering at the slightest movement, and then of course there was the smoked sausage, hard and firm in contrast, which the machine cut in uniform paper-thin slices.

She had already overspent in this first shop, but after all, she reminded herself, it was the weekend treat and why shouldn't she be self-indulgent? She liked everything about food, the shopping and selecting, the small decisions, the preparation and of course the actual cooking, knowing exactly how to achieve the flavours she wanted—and as for the eating, well, she enjoyed herself as much as the others, of that she was quite sure.

The herrings were clear of eye, firm and silver-blue. She bought a kilo. The shrimps were expensive, but she couldn't resist tasting one while they cut the middle part of a smoked eel for her; the tail and head someone else could have. She was a good shopper and respected for it, that was certain, but at the same time she knew she irritated the customers behind her in the queue, as she always insisted on taking her time, tasting, feeling, sniffing. She finally succumbed to a few hectos of the pale pink shrimps, just for the flavour and for a bit of decoration round the plates.

The bags were getting quite heavy, but never mind, she was used to carrying things. At the vegetable stall she again had time to reject, select, taste, thumb the tomatoes while nobody was looking. As the day wore on the queues were longer, but nothing of that kind worried her. Yes, she would certainly have the new carrots; they looked like gaudy seed advertisements. The bunched-up dainty little sugar-peas in their pretty boxes, the red ribbons round them, made her think of Christmas presents. And there was the cauliflower, which was a luxury, but thinking of the cheese sauce over the intricate flowerlets finally decided her to buy two of them.

She had not forgotten the aquavit, the strong beer that Dad preferred and the sweet punch for the coffee, and she had taken a stout canvas bag for the purpose. Portfolios and overnight cases were being stocked full around her; it was a busy day at any branch of the liquor monopoly. If a customer looked at all dubious, bank-notes were fingered and put up to the light. She was always slightly apprehensive that the red light would go on when her turn came. So far it had only happened once and then of course she had had no identity papers with her. It had been really embarrassing, but in the end they had trusted her looks and let her buy. It was silly, but she always felt guilty standing there in one of the long queues and wished that Dad would take over that particular chore.

All of a sudden she began feeling quite faint with hunger and started to look forward to selecting the open sandwich she had decided to have for lunch — and perhaps even, with the coffee, a piece of the chocolate cake which she and Nils always chose when they went out together, so light and fruity a concoction that it melted in the mouth. She smiled to herself at the thought of them both; they were hopeless when it came to sweets and cakes, and couldn't help indulging each other.

She chose the roast beef sandwich with the mayonnaise, the pickled melon and the crisply fried onions.

Her feet were tired, her arms were aching and she was over-excited by the morning's shopping. She enjoyed the act of chewing the sandwich and taking dainty sips of coffee and not talking to anyone. It was restful to let the eyes wander and the mind go blank. The whole system of the shop pleased her. She had liked choosing the delicately laid-out sandwich, taking her time, and what a hard choice it had been. She poured her own coffee and paid a girl with an inscrutable mask of a face behind a cash register. The operation was simple, there was nobody she felt she had to talk to, the service was impersonal and everything spotlessly shining on brightly lit surfaces, and the softly filtered music was soporific.

She was beginning to feel soft and funny again in the pit of

her stomach as she thought how very lucky she was, with Dad
fit and in a good job, Svea married and well settled; perhaps she
had an idea that all was not quite well between her and Tor,
who seemed rather a bore, but she didn't really want to inquire
into their lives, as Svea never said a word and anyway her
grandchildren were well-behaved and she enjoyed boasting
about them.

And then of course there was Nils, her favourite and first-
born. After the initial disappointment of his not being a girl,
which she had dreamt of and hoped for, she had really relished
him and not wanted any more children. Svea had been a mistake; even physically it had all been wrong. She was squarely
built, tough and tomboyish and even as a baby without charm,
while Nils had been pretty, the kind of child people stopped to
admire; they wanted to pinch his cheek when she took him out
in the pram. He was so affectionate to everyone and especially
to her—how proud she had been of him, what a good son he
had turned out to be, considerate, always thinking of others, so
reliable.

She read his letter again as she had the cake and thought of
him at each swallow. Yes, she was indeed lucky.

With the dye running streakily down his face, he began to look
like an Indian warrior preparing for ritual, and he felt suitably
solemn and ceremonial as he brushed it on with an old toothbrush.

He was getting the effect he was after—his hair, otherwise a
light mousy blond, was now tinted a vivid red. He only hoped
that what the packet said about washing it off was correct,
otherwise it would be rather hard to explain at work on Monday.
He put in the largest of his rollers and settled down to dyeing
the extra hairpiece which he hoped could give the sweeping,
bouncy, Veronica Lake style that he had once admired, but the
fineness of his hair did not make it easy. There would have to
be plenty of back-combing and lacquer.

Mother's hair was just the same, it took enormous trouble to get her wispy, uncontrollable strands into any kind of shape. She liked him doing her hair, though, and made purring pigeon-like noises of contentment when he brushed it. He was certainly gentler, she had said, than any of the hairdressers she visited for her yearly perm.

He wished he were better at needlework and was sorry now not to have made more effort at school. He had not dared to admit enjoying it because of the teasing it produced in class. All the same he was making headway with the dress and liked thinking of the effect of the rich purple velvet against the red hair. It was simple enough in style except for the colour and the big puff sleeves, so he had decided to work it up a bit by sewing pearls round the neckline and opening a slit in the skirt. The final touches were the bouquet of violets tied to the waist and the white gloves.

Svea's old black patent-leather shoes would have to do. The heels were a bit high for comfortable dancing, but after a while he could go slightly mad, kick them off and dance in stockinged feet. He thought of Rita Hayworth. His stomach was rumbling and slightly painful after the laxative he had taken in the morning. He would try not to eat until the party, which was to be in Lola's flat as usual; she had a large, modern, sophisticated apartment, very different from what any of them could offer.

Apart from her job—she worked as a photographer for one of the dailies—Lola had private money. She was certainly a curiosity—had even been married once for a couple of months and told the most hair-raising stories about it. She was generous with her money and a find, he supposed, but the hangers-on were innumerable. She could be cosy and homely if she liked, but there was often a touch of sardonic humour which spoilt the atmosphere of friendliness she tried to create. She was always dressed in a well-cut black suit to disguise her plumpness, wore a man's white shirt and tie almost as a kind of uniform.

Lola tried to have steady girls but they never seemed to last long, apart from Alice who had now been with her for almost half a year, for which everyone was duly grateful. The parties had become more peaceful, more like family reunions. But if for some reason they found her in a bad mood the evening was half ruined from the start. She soon became loud-mouthed and domineering, often really ugly, when they all wanted was to enjoy themselves quietly.

From time to time he bent double over the sewing, wishing he had not taken that pill, remembering with a pain that came in waves the time he had stolen the bar of chocolate from the bathroom cupboard, all too soon discovering that it was laxative. Mother had worried so and not once told him off, even with the frightful mess. Only afterwards had they cried with laughter together. Sweets, after all, were a passion they shared and he had been forgiven.

Later he couldn't resist the lovely little cold snacks that were really for Sunday, cheeses wrapped in uncrinkled silver paper, strong-smelling and soft, radishes lying in ice-cubes, pink and pointed with spring-like leaves, a plastic bag of shrimps filled with roe, a few tins of meatballs, of course. He thought of the ones that Mother was probably making at this very moment and felt nostalgic. She was bound to have them tonight, as always.

He opened a tin and was at once disappointed. Lying tightly packed in brown jelly, they looked almost square in shape, a far cry from the perfect spheres they used to roll together. He crushed some with a fork on a piece of battered hard bread and had a cup of tea with it. Then he put a cake in the oven, this being his contribution to the party, and it soon became more homely. The smell of melting chocolate was sweet and over-powering and he felt excited in anticipation of the party.

She had sharpened all her favourite knives for the preparations. Neatly she cut the heads off the herrings, split their middles expertly, and with a quick flick of her finger pulled out the brittle backbone in one go, and they were lying open and raw on the scrubbed slab of wood, waiting only to be filled with chopped parsley.

While she cut the curly, deep-green herb, she thought of summer and grass and their picnics when they all cycled to the lake, and she thought of the Sunday when Per had drowned so unnecessarily but perhaps all the same for the best — who could tell now? There had been a strange animosity between the boys and the only times when Nils had been at all difficult were when Per was born and in the year preceding the accident. He had clung to her with desperation and shown a nasty streak of jealousy. Dad had been very strict with him now and again. Odd how Svea was free of any similar feelings.

After Per's death it was almost as if he were happy. He was at once more obedient and more devoted to her than ever. Yes, all the difficulties had come to an end, it seemed, except that he still wanted her breast now and then. All through his first six years she had plenty of milk because of Svea and then Per in quick succesion; there was always some left over for him. Dad said he was a bit old for it, but she felt it could really do him no harm. And he was difficult to refuse when he stood between her knees and put his cheek to her breast, undoing a button or two and then looking up at her in such a sweet way. She had always enjoyed nursing the children and was secretly pleased that he still wanted it. How could she help liking the sensation of his eager hands as she gave him the breast? So they were both content.

It only became a problem when the milk all of a sudden stopped because of the shock of Per's death. She told him; he did not understand. He cried bitterly and went off into corners and sulked for hours. So finally, taking pity on him, she put him on her knee and felt a mixture of guilt and elation as he played with her and bit into her nipples.

It was only the incident which made her give it up completely. A neighbour burst into the room without warning one day, was duly shocked and said so. After all the boy was getting on for seven. So despite his tears and tantrums she was firm.

She felt warm and comfortable as she stood in her well-ordered kitchen, her hands smeared with the mixture of raw meat, breadcrumbs and eggs. She slapped the meat delicately from hand to hand and then with strong fingers divided it into small round uniform shapes. She liked touching things, to be intimately connected with the world and its objects and felt totally satisfied with life as it was, waddling between the stove and the working surface, cleaning up every dish as she used it so as always to have a shining surface of aluminium in front of her.

She knew and had been told that she did far too much unnecessary work, her eye catching every particle of dust and every drop that spoilt the glitter. But what did it matter? She felt there was plenty of time and anyway she seemed always to have hours to spare. But somehow peeling the onions made her feel uneasy. They were particularly strong for that time of year and even the sugar-lump between the teeth seemed not to help. The tears were rolling down her cheeks, so much so that she felt obliged to be unhappy about something, and finally for no reason, except the purely physical fact of the onion, she sat down at the kitchen table and had a really good cry with a considerable degree of pleasure. How she wished that Nils wasn't so far away; she never saw him enough and would miss his dear face tonight. He was always so gay and spirited. There was a great gap in her life.

She pulled herself out of the gloom by making a strong cup of coffee and getting busy again. She had let herself go and been silly and childish. While sipping the cooling coffee and dunking bread in it, she watched television. An ugly contortion of the face caught her attention, as she memorized the things still left to be done, the best porcelain and glass to be taken out and dusted, the silver polished. She had no idea what the programme was all about, not having really looked or listened, but she thought the expression was of a wounded man in a war somewhere. She tried to put the hideous vision out of her mind; it made her think of the minor illnesses Nils had suffered as a child, for he had been delicate and worried her a lot.

So once more she started to feel ill at ease and, getting to her feet, she dusted the carnations that stood stiffly in the cut-glass vase. They almost looked real and certainly she preferred them to fresh-cut flowers that with her never seemed to last at all. And then she watered the pot plants that stood queueing on the window-sill, all turned to the sparse winter light.

There was still plenty of time before she need begin to cook. The afternoon moved slowly and, as the sombre grey turned into a night sky towards four o'clock, she felt sleepy and wished that the evening was over. Sitting stiffly upright with a magazine and an aching back, she found herself nodding.

It was an especially hard frost that evening. The trees seemed to sparkle messages to one another and everything was electric, every footfall a noisy reminder of life.

He laughed to himself at the thought of what the stuffy citizens would say if they knew what was hidden beneath that expensive-looking fur hat on his head. He still had the curlers in his dyed hair, which after all had turned out a more vivid red than he expected. Otherwise he looked immaculate in his good, almost new, suede winter-coat with the fur collar, carrying the embarrassingly smart overnight case with his gold initials almost sparkling. The well-wrapped small bunch of flowers and the cake-box completed the picture of a respectable gentleman visiting his friends for the weekend. It was a hilarious thought.

There was a lot of hectic running to and fro, as before a children's party or a school play, and Lola was in a foul mood. She didn't greet him properly, she snatched the presents out of his hands with almost a snarl. He tried hard to overcome his disappointment, and was gallant and overdid his flattery so much that even she was aware of it. Though she expected it from them all, she still had a curious yardstick that made her realize total dishonesty — even if, as now, it sprang as much from fear as anything else.

In a sense Nils felt that the preparations, the making up, doing one another's hair, admiring, flirting, the lifting of eyebrows, the screams of surprise, were really the best part of the evening. The only remotely conservative people were Walter and Gert, who played at being married and always wore the same old boring court dresses. Their rusting tiaras had too many stones missing and they were stingy with their accessories. You simply could not wear boots with a black velvet dress. They were both typesetters on Lola's paper and had reached a bickering stage in their relationship, flirting in a childish, unserious way to make each other jealous, but always ending up in each other's arms half-sloshed and crying.

Lola filled their glasses while encouraging them to be more and more idiotic. Her laugh irritated Nils — she only laughed *at* them — and her eyebrows were raised sarcastically, as if that were their permanent expression.

They all tried to outdo one another in camp as they combed their wigs, stuffed their breasts, applied their make-up. Olle was a scream in a short spotted sunsuit, which looked indecent above his hairy legs, a blond curly wig, dark glasses and a straw hat. Tage, as helpless as ever, had to be fitted out from the left-overs and a suitcase of silks, chiffons and ribbons which Olle had borrowed from the window-dressing department. By the time someone pinned a curly fringe to Tage's sleek pommaded hair everyone was in stitches. Hasse looked magnificent in a Spanish mantilla and frilly dress which he had hired for the occasion. His was a real transformation. The blue-black wig suited him so well that it was impossible to remember the receding strands beneath it. And all the time he assumed ridiculous postures, flirted atrociously over his fan and announced at the top of his voice how mad he felt and how much in love with himself he was.

When Alice let herself in a couple of hours late with a girl she had picked up, the atmosphere deteriorated, though nothing was said. Everyone avoided looking at Lola and Alice — it was too discomfiting — so Nils concentrated on himself, feeling pretty and elegant and cool, his hair covering one of his eyes. It was long enough to swish round and lay over one shoulder; he could play coy and unattainable. Everyone, already tipsy, was pretending to be gay. The party was on.

The dog barked, clawed the door and started whining long before Svea and family arrived. Almost pushing her over as she opened the door, he rushed straight to the kitchen, knowing where his titbits awaited him. He didn't bother to greet her; he only ate. She had divided feelings about this dog, which was at once spoilt and badly treated, being fed all the wrong foods, never getting enough exercise, so that it was clumsy and greedy and full of complaints. She felt sorry for the animal, yet couldn't quite bear to look at his runny eyes and the stomach that sagged so badly. There was not much left of the pedigree dog he had once been.

They stamped their feet and got rid of most of the slush on the iron grill outside, clearing the rest with the hard brush just inside the front door, where she had put a mat for just that purpose. There was a lot of activity with boots and galoshes, woollen drawers were rolled up and put into pockets and sleeves, hats put on racks, coats on hangers. The hall seemed full of clothes, noise, breathing. Nothing was said, only orders were given, and shrieks, whispers, cries and grumbles were the reply from children, dog and husband.

The children were overwrought from several Christmas parties, not to say bored with the prospect of the usual Saturday evening with their grandparents. Tor and Svea spoke disconcertingly with complaints in their voices, looking past each other, and there were big silences ahead. She knew the evening would drag, but then she was used to it. It was still a pleasant change in the routine; she still had a silly, large idea of Saturday night being special. In the past Nils had certainly helped to make it so with his chatter and gaiety.

A touch of discontent, of disappointment, was lodged in her stomach; she could almost pinpoint it. It wasn't exactly painful, but it weighed her down. She gave the children the messy old button-box which they loved, a lifetime of shirts, dresses, coats, baby-frocks, dreams. Svea and Tor were bickering over some trivial matters. Dad was his usual self, timid, never interfering, stuck in front of the set which was playing at its highest volume, with the purpose of filling in the dull gaps that were inevitable.

Svea kept her company in the kitchen, while she put the last touches to the food, and asked for Nils's latest news. Well, there had been the New Year sale and the store detectives had caught three highly respectable women: most embarrassing — and such trifles they had taken. Nils had said they must be ill and was sorry for them, which of course, they agreed, was typical of him. They felt it was disgusting and refused to understand it. Then one of the young girl assistants had killed herself with an overdose — quite pretty too. They decided it was shameful — just to think of the poor parents and what they had to live with afterwards and the neighbours. They blamed the girl without knowing anything about her.

Nils was going to a party that Saturday night with a girl-friend, but nothing serious, he had added, so she needn't worry. He was sad the holiday was over and had been so short, he missed her cooking and of course he would love to be with them now rather than at the party. She remembered every little word of the letter. She had read it often enough and eagerly gave all its details. It lifted her spirits a little and she was feeling quite contented again when she told them that dinner was ready. It was six thirty.

During the cold buffet they still kept admiring one another — what else was there to talk about? — and while pretending to be interested in what they said and did, he felt false through and through. Surely it must show. He felt his face was falling apart and his voice was unsure and affected, the whole thing both depressed and shamed him. The only answer was to drink and keep up the pretence of gaiety. He already knew how rotten he would feel in the morning — this burden of guilt mixed with a hangover.

Olle was dancing with Walter who had totally lost control of himself, his voice slurred with drink, his face a badly fitting puzzle. Gert was fuming silently, drinking fast, hands shaking, eyes filled with tears. Hasse was still in love with his outfit and could not stop looking in the mirror as he waltzed about the room.

Lola, beginning to lose her temper, confided in a high-pitched voice to Nils what she would do to the cow who was seducing Alice. They agreed she was in the wrong company with her ill-fitting blue woollen dress, her piggy little eyes behind thick-rimmed glasses. Completely at a loss on her arrival, she had now lost herself in Alice and was just a mess, a rather woolly blancmange with sweat dripping from her face and in wet patches under her arms, sitting with a grin and fondling Alice, who had stopped caring; Lola just wanted revenge, revenge for something that Nils didn't quite understand and had no particular wish to know about.

Then suddenly Lola rose and rolled across the room like a machine destroying everything in its way. Bottles fell, tables swayed, bodies were pushed back. She cleared a straight path to the girl and lifted her as if she were a paper doll. It all happened so quickly that no one had time to protest or interfere. Almost at arm's length she carried the limp body to the bedroom and locked the door firmly. It was very quiet and very uncomfortable. Someone burped. There was no sound from the other side of the door.

At length Alice, sour at being locked out, walked unsteadily to the door of the bedroom. The mood had gone rotten. Olle playing the clown tried clumsily to cheer her up, but it was thought better to leave them to it. She sat down outside the door with a bottle of wine which she swigged heavily as she kicked the door loudly and cursed. Meanwhile they took pictures of one another which they hoped Lola would develop. Usually she did so the same evening, but tonight it seemed unlikely. They treasured their fine collection of half-pornographic shots of themselves.

Nils had assumed a languid pose. The split of his dress nearly

reached his thighs; it was just possible to see that he wasn't a
girl. Olle worked it up to a fine stand, excitement mounted,
Gert and Walter, reconciled, went off to a corner, Olle had to
have it, he said, but they all wanted to preserve their make-up
and hairstyles and Olle was a rough one. He went sulking
round the room threatening to jerk himself off and getting very
little sympathy, while Tage and Hasse danced a slow, old-
fashioned foxtrot.

Nils saw how it all happened. He was sitting on the other
side of the room helping himself to some more fruit salad and
cream. Olle had edged his way to Alice and was looking at her
dishevelled state. She wore a miniskirt showing knickers as
tight round her bottom as well-fitting gloves. He slumped
down on the chair next to her and muttered a few words. He
was aware of a vague reaction from the bundle on the floor
and he saw her laugh. Olle took out his more-than-average
cock and started jerking it in front of her while pushing her
with his foot, and Nils decided the moment was suddenly a
nightmare, he wasn't there or it wasn't happening. She pulled
him down and, though surprised, he followed all the instruc-
tions she began to yell at him for the benefit of Lola, from the
moment of peeling her knickers off to the final ejaculation,
when she let out groan upon groan of lust, anger and frustra-
tion which shattered the room.

Tage and Hasse had edged nearer and were standing stock
still. Gert and Walter were tittering from their corner. So that
no one should notice Nils moved slowly towards Lola's work-
room; he felt violently sick, he had to get away from it.

Then the flat was all of a sudden full of running, screaming
people, doors opening and shutting, a total involvement of
everyone but him; for he had crept into the quiet room and
noiselessly closed the door. He felt unreal, ghostly, as he padded
around the room for a moment, then sank down in front of the
blank television screen. He was trembling all over. He heard
his name being shouted once or twice, but he felt immovable,
he knew his legs would not carry him even if he tried.

F

So this was what it was like to suffer from shock, he thought, his teeth chattering in the overheated room. Despite his disgust he could not block out what he had seen, every move seemed to be cruelly imprinted on his brain, he was in a cold panic. There was a bottle of whisky at hand and he, who never touched hard liquor, drank it like a draught of water. It seemed to settle his stomach and nerves a little, anyway numbed his senses, but it took none of the sickness away. When all was quiet again he heard his heart beat so loudly that it frightened him. He switched on the television; the images were blurred, they were talking a language he did not know, but at least it was a sound to make him forget his own body. The room swam. Objects seemed to move, nothing was still, even the carpet kept on changing patterns. He felt irrecoverably lost.

The evening had turned out more disappointing than usual. What was wrong with her? The food, over which she had taken so much trouble, seemed tasteless and dull. The children had been as naughty as they were allowed, Dad his silent self; Svea and Tor had bickered their way through the evening and the dog had snored loudly for hours. What was wrong with her?

Perhaps it was a premonition of illness. She felt uneasy. They watched the quiz programme after dinner, which she always thought funny because of the comedian who chaired it. But tonight she didn't laugh once. Perhaps she had worked too hard lately, she felt suddenly old and worn-out, and wished the evening were over, but it was only nine o'clock and they certainly wouldn't leave until well after ten. It was hard to sit still, so after a few lame protests from the others she left for the kitchen, her own domain.

The smells from the food still lingered; and though on a normal evening she would have liked the peace, the warmth, today it was slightly nauseating. She was obviously not well, yet she could locate no particular pain in her body. She wrapped up some scraps for the dog in silver foil and put them into a plastic bag, fingered the evening paper but didn't want to read it, swept the floor for the third time that day. Back with the others, she noticed that the children had made a mess of the fruit bowl and she thanked them silently for giving her something to do.

When Dad and Tor sat down for a game of cards, she could count on at least an hour before they left. Svea would take out the dog, who had been barking for ten minutes by the door. She herself would make coffee, the children would get noisier and pull the chain in the bathroom too loudly and too often. This was all written in the stars, a routine impossible to change, it seemed.

The relief was immense when they left, despite a lingering touch of guilt at having wanted to get rid of them. Dad soon fell asleep over his patience. She looked at his sunken, exhausted face and thought how ugly he was — and again was surprised at her thoughts. The television was still on and it was almost midnight; there was some sort of late film in a foreign language. She did not bother to fetch her glasses so that she could read the titles, it was enough to sit and look at people moving, something to hold her interest and prevent her thinking of herself. She was in a curious mood which she neither liked nor knew how to handle, except by pretending that it did not exist.

Dad woke up at some point, smoked a pipe, snorted, pottered, ate a few titbits from the fridge and said nothing. The only voices came from the people on the screen. She had no idea what the whole thing was about. She heard him go into the bedroom and put on his record, the scratched Caruso singing *O sole mio*. She had never asked him why he cried every night to that strange voice; she had never thought much of it herself. Perhaps she didn't really want to know what odd worlds he was hiding, perhaps she really didn't want to know what kind of man he was. She fed him, slept in the same room, washed his smelly socks, and she felt for the first time that she didn't know him at all. When she thought of it, the fact that they had had children together startled her; it was indecent, she felt nothing for him, never had. She knew how he was crying into his handkerchief silently and she joined him crying with heavy sighs. It was the second time that day and again she was astonished at herself, for it was unnatural; she usually cried more with joy and laughter than from sadness and hurt.

In silence they went to bed. There was nothing more to talk about. He was soon snoring evenly beside her; he never stirred in his sleep. She lay for a long time open-eyed and anxious, not knowing why.

The room seemed to have been torn apart by intruders: broken glass, spilt wine like blood oozing, plates of uneaten food already smelling mouldy in the mugginess of the flat. Otherwise the atmosphere was dead and he had a real fright when he caught himself in the mirror – an apparition, unhealthy, white, almost transparent. He tripped over draperies, glasses, flowers; everything in the room seemed broken, even doors were hanging off their hinges.

Lola was lying shipwrecked on top of the bedclothes. Somebody had been at work on her. Her clothes were torn, her hair was a tangled mess, her face puffy with tears, and he thought someone had given her one in the eye. Painful sounds came from her, though she appeared to be fast asleep. Her shirt had been ripped and was hanging off her in ribbons like a carnival costume. Her brassiere was round her waist and her pants were missing, so that she looked disgusting and her shaven triangle frightened him. Her breasts, heavy and brown-nippled, looked tempting though they were totally different from Mother's; hers had been like sweet warm dough with their small pink upstanding tips which he had loved so.

And then a terrifying desire filled his whole body, he felt himself trembling again, he had gooseflesh all over and his head was aching. Everything seemed unbearable if somehow he could not take those objects lying there waiting for him. He thought of that lady neighbour who had come upon one of their intimate moments and started to hate her all over again, it was she who had started the rot; surely he had been happy until then. He hated Lola with almost the same intensity as he edged nearer.

She did not by any means smell like Mother, but her nipple had a somewhat similar taste and, although it was so long ago, the familiar way of caressing and biting into it came naturally to him. In the mirror opposite the bed he saw with excitement his long red hair falling over Lola's breasts, his long purple dress glowing in the half-light, his painted mask. He kneaded and clawed and sucked her until he had a pain in the groin, the same kind of pain he had experienced with Mother, but now he had an erection that seemed to throb in his whole body.

He never quite knew when she actually woke up or how long he had been feverishly working on her, but he felt her hands pulling him closer, pinning him to her. He tried to wrench free in order to get back the clasp of the breasts and whimpered for them, she understood and let him do it, but then he felt her hands all over him, searching for his slit, finding it, soon moving into his underpants and pulling him. He panicked; the whole bed seemed to turn round, he felt himself go limp, then he held both her breasts in his hands and vomited all over her.

Her fury made her strong. She hauled him out, cursing, sobbing, hit him with whatever came to hand; and he couldn't defend himself, lacked the strength or even the will to fight back. The room smelt of sick, he felt like dying, he could not remember how or when he got out of her clutches. The only far-away memory was of a kitchen knife, a scrap of carpet, a pool of blood and then a sharp light in his eyes.

He was still in the evening dress when he woke up in hospital. The nurses stared at his hennaed hair, which must have looked somewhat unreal in the strong sunlight that flooded into the room and bounced off the walls, making his eyes smart. They took his underwear off in a telling silence and he heard them whispering about the good quality of the silk and the heavy lace attached to the wide camiknickers. Part of Mother's trousseau, they had only been worn on the wedding day, then put in a box and stored. He had known she would never miss them.

They washed his face and peeled off one eyelash; the other he had lost. They had difficulty removing all the make-up, their rags turning brown and blue as they rubbed. He felt too embarrassed to talk. In any case what could he say? He was cold with shame.

It was equally embarrassing to fetch all the odds and ends when he was discharged. He claimed them without looking anyone in the eye. They were tittering in the corridors as he left, looking so very respectable with his rolled umbrella and homburg which Olle had delivered to the hospital. He was weak-headed as he stepped into the street, where a journalist who had been waiting in a car rushed at him like a bull. He knew the man vaguely. He felt at once violent and sick and he was still shaking in the taxi he had hailed after running down the street, through the traffic, with the journalist shouting inaudibly behind him.

He was shivering and perspiring heavily when he entered the flat where the dust lay thick. The telephone rang almost at once, he jumped in fright, but let it ring on. He sat in darkness all evening, answering neither telephone nor doorbell. Too scared to move, he had pins and needles all over his body; it was a deep and desperate childish fear that he felt getting hold of him.

After a sleepless night, still sitting in the same chair with his hat and coat on, he summoned up enough courage to ring Olle. He would go and visit his Mother and get in touch on his return. Yes, he was fine, really all right, needed no help, didn't want to talk. Did he know there were rumours that it might be in the papers? Lola was mad at them and wanted revenge. Meanwhile, Tage was trying to get hold of the photographs and was willing to pay for them.

He went to the bathroom and back to his chair again, he had no strength for more and no thought in his head and his throat was dry. All emotion had vanished. Hours passed. The phone rang from time to time, making him slightly nervous for a while; it began to grow dark again, he must try to get some hold on himself. He forced down some yoghurt, which tasted foul, and was surprised to find that he was still wearing the hat and thick overcoat though he had been frozen all along. He knew he ought to ring Mother, but it was impossible. She would worry over missing his Sunday call, so he took some tranquillizers the hospital had given him and sat down to write.

It was hard holding a pen, even harder to compose a letter, harder still to spell properly, and hardest of all to make the letter sound just as usual. The drugs made him sleepy and he dozed off now and then. It took him until midnight to finish a bad letter and it took another couple of tranquillizers before he dared go down and post it. Getting back home and looking for the keys in his pocket were not easy either; it all seemed cumbersome. It was with great relief that he closed the door behind him again. He had seen no one. He was grateful for the raging snowstorm that almost rendered him invisible.

He made a large plate of porridge, as he only had to pour boiling water over the flakes. He could not chew, but to let things glide down the gullet seemed just possible. He heaped spoons of sugar and syrup over the steaming pudding that emerged and sprayed ice-cold milk on top. He made two large helpings and in between had the brandy which he kept for emergencies, and he felt warm for the first time. Then he fell asleep in the bath until the cold water woke him. Exhausted, he slept for a solid twelve hours. And then he made up his mind. It was Thursday. On Friday he wrote to her:

Dear Mother, I've had a couple of very busy days and I don't want you to worry about anything. The flat is paid up to the next quarter, starting April 1st. You should try to sell it on the black market. You will get a good price even in this god-forsaken place. I worked all yesterday and well into the night clearing it out. You will find it to your satisfaction, I hope. As you know, there isn't much furniture, but you and Svea will have to share it as best you can, although I would want you to have the old rocking-chair which you've always liked—it's quite valuable—if you can find a place for it, of course. Also the antique chest and the rhinestone bracelet I did at home last year, at least the stones will fetch something. There is 6,586 crowns in the Savings Book and I have paid almost 600 crowns into the Holiday Club at the shop, which you should be able to claim back. The only other things of value are my clothes I suppose. Items: 1 new umbrella, a fur hat (mink), 2 homburgs, very good quality and new, 1 new pair of pigskin gloves (never worn), 1 summer suit (also never worn), 1 suitcase (leather) from the sales (you will have to change the initials, it can be done), 1 gold bracelet worth about 400 crowns. Don't get cheated on these things. The rest is in very good order really and my suede overcoat with the mink collar was new last year. The tax has all been paid up and there are no bills. I bought some presents for the children's next birthdays—you will find them wrapped up at the top of the wardrobe. I bought a crocodile bag for you —I know you always wanted one, and it's there too, with a silk tie for Dad and a pin, the pearl is real, and a bracelet for Svea. I hope you will like the presents and forgive me.

I don't want a church burial so I suppose the best thing is to be cremated. If you want to send flowers I would like some lily of the valley, that is if you can get them now (there is 250 crowns in cash, in my wallet). But please don't put yourself out as it doesn't really matter. I have thought about all this a lot these last days and I do want to be forgotten as quickly as possible. It's very hard to explain anything. I'm very sorry if I hurt you by what I am doing, but believe me, please, when I say I'm doing what is best for all of us.

I hope you are very well and that you and Dad will continue to have a happy life together.

I am your loving son.

They must have locked the gates at six. He had heard them clanging shut. Now he was hiding behind a sort of gardener's tool-shed, knee-deep in rotted frozen flowers and wreaths that smelt even through the snow of death and decay. It was pitch black with not a single star to light the paths that crossed one another between the graves. He was feeling like a lost traveller on a curious expedition.

They illuminated the big cross on the hill at eight o'clock; he heard the bell chime and moved towards it. The snow on the paths was frozen hard, but the graves still had a thick softish layer topped by a hard crust. He passed a newly dug grave where the earth seemed rich and warm. There were also plenty of fresh flowers on top of a lot of greenery. It made an inviting bed.

It suited his purpose well. Also, from here he could just catch a glimpse of the cross between fir trees if he lay down, and the man had not long been dead so he felt less lonely. He was walking round the graves in a kind of trance, keeping himself warm; it was not a cold night, but he wanted to make absolutely sure he would be snug when he finally stretched out. The thought of the pills so carefully wrapped up in his hankie comforted. Perhaps the doctor had been his friend after all. It made him think of the people he loved, but he suddenly realized to his surprise that he loved no one, not even her, only himself. Everyone seemed so remote that they had no faces any more. On the other hand he felt curiously alive, his body tingling. He had never felt more real or happier and had no idea why it should be so just now. He could see everything so clearly and there were no more problems.

Large flakes of snow started to fall gently around him, which made him cry a little bit, but it was so much better than he had thought. He swallowed the pills with the help of some snow. The bed was soft, he was warm under his thick coat, his heart beat with excitement. He had never been so aware of the throbbing comfort of his body before, and at that moment he loved life but did not mind never waking up. The flowers made him giddy, he sank his head deep into them and even found a wreath of lily of the valley to cling to. He would look so pretty when they found him covered with the snow that was already beginning to suffocate him. He was truly happy, yes, so happy and forgotten for always.

He seemed to be on fire. There was nothing but pain. He was vaguely aware of thinking processes somewhere within, but it was all confusion, mixed up with this all-enveloping pain. Surely this was not what death was supposed to be like, surely it was nothingness, the big sleep. Later he became aware of textures and far-away voices and it frightened him to realize that he had a body still and he started to shake. Someone was holding him down firmly and they were hurting him.

Again much later he realized that he was in hospital once more. The smells were the first thing he was conscious of, then the whiteness around him; then he recognized the presence of nurses, who seemed to move in a fog at a great distance, mouthing words at him, words he did not understand. Sleep was all he desired and they gave it to him — the needles they put into his body made him groggy and again and again he fainted away from the world, only to wake up every so often to a sharp glimpse of it. His parents, stony-faced, bewildered. But he couldn't keep his eyes open ... and then, again half-awake, he saw Hasse gesticulating at Mother, and he wanted to stop him but lacked the strength to lift his arms and could not remember how to use his voice. Later he cried. He had not realized a man could be so full of tears. So many needles had gone into him that his whole body seemed an open sore, and his head was a whirlpool from which there was no escape, and there were thunderous noises, and echoes of them, and when he opened his eyes, violent patterns flashed at him; then deep oblivion again. In the end he was limp, wet, totally exhausted.

Years seemed to have passed before he could patch together what had happened. He was told how the dogs had found his snowed-up body, indeed it was the snow which had preserved him. He tried to tell the staff that he didn't want to see anyone. He had even begun hating Mother; her face had sunk away, she was an ugly old woman whom he didn't want to know. She came and went and there was no communication between them. He used to feign sleep most of the time.

But there came a Sunday when to his horror the whole family arrived, dressed in black as for a funeral, ludicrously out of place. When he dared to look again, his eyes tiny slits, they were grouped silently round his bed with solemn faces; the scene was so ridiculous that he broke the silence with a great burst of laughter. It was the first sign of anything human happening in him, but it was such an unexpected and terrifying laugh that Mother instantly began crying and the others rose to their feet in panic. The nurse hustled them away and gave him a sedative and he sailed off to sleep once more with a curiously satisfied smile on his face, as if he had at last got rid of them.

They had brought him three tulips, two narcissi and one lonely rose which was wilting. There was a curt note from Svea saying that Father had to go back to work so Mother had to leave as well. They all hoped he would be better soon. Mother was a bit tired from the trip, so they also hoped he would understand if she didn't write at once.

He could not guess how long he had been in hospital. One day Olle told him; it was two months. Not only the local press but even the big dailies had taken up the small-town scandal, interviewing Lola, printing pictures of them all. Olle grew bored with him when he did not react to the gossip. Pretending to be tired, he just turned his back.

He was moved to a convalescent home twenty kilometres out of town. It was easy to forget his past and he succeeded quite well in killing his emotional life. He had his own room, which was as empty as himself, and he really felt nothing as he stared at the wooden ceiling for hours on end before going to sleep. He wished only that they would leave him in peace. The doctors, the psychiatrist, the priest, all tried to involve him in life again, but he fought them hard. All he accepted were the food, the pills, the sleep that was ordered. He made no friends and felt best by himself. It was good to be staring out of windows, letting oneself sink into nothingness.

They could do very little for him. The institution was a sort of halfway house to the lunatic asylum, which was not for him, they said. He wondered what was.

He signed all the papers for his pension money. They exchanged his flat for a similar one in a town some hundred kilometres to the north, where he had never been. That was his only wish: not to be known.

The welfare people were there waiting for him. They left with promises to return soon to visit him. The view on one side was of distant mountains; and close at hand some large pines almost brushed his windows. On the kitchen side were the usual playgrounds, roads and car-parks and the main highway into town. The whole thing was so familiar that all night he had a vague feeling of discomfort.

The first month he did nothing to it. He let the stacked-up furniture get dustier and didn't even bother to make up the bed. The local priest appeared on a sudden visit and told him to pull himself together, meet people and so forth. He was ludicrous in his enthusiasm and belief in mankind; Nils wanted to snarl at him like a mad dog and bite him in the leg. At length, however, he succumbed and went along to the home day, where other misfits like himself and old idiots sat sipping the weak coffee and dunking sweet home-baked cakes. It felt like a return to nursery school with the reading aloud and the singing and the piano-playing. The patronizing hands on his shoulder seemed to burn all the way into him, but he found himself going back; there was always something for him to do, they began to rely on him. Where before he had been totally inactive, he now became the opposite. He was a model of tidiness, kept himself and the flat spotlessly clean, prepared large meals for himself three times a day, put on weight and lost almost all his hair. Within a year he was unrecognizable. He was pleased with the transformation, though disgusted when he looked in a mirror.

He decorated things for the Christmas bazaar; his designs had not improved, but they seemed to like it. He served coffee after the services several times a week, he blew up balloons at the children's parties, he took the priest's baby out in the pram, did the collections, sang in the choir, all without a single thought in his head. His time was the night, for his dream world had changed. He used to say he never dreamt, but now he couldn't stop and always went early to bed, longing for sleep, for dreams, for fantasies. She was always there, but young, smiling, pretty, so different from Mother but yet still her. He no longer felt any need to get in touch with her, because she was now his for ever and ever.

They never talked about him and one by one all the photographs disappeared. It was as if she were dusting him out of her life. One small picture she kept, though, at the bottom of her sewing-basket. He was one year old. In the long-haired rug the body looked fragile and so white. It had been taken when it was the fashion to photograph naked babies. She could somehow look at that picture without being disappointed or hurt.

Dad had been totally bewildered at first by the goings-on; and later he had turned to a blind hatred of which she had never thought him capable. He had insisted that the boy's name should never be mentioned again after the disgrace. She cried a lot then, but had to give in. He knew her feelings but kept his mouth tightly shut, and when of an evening, he at his patience, she at her needlework, their eyes met suddenly by mistake, they turned away pained and embarrassed.

Svea, pretending shock, had secretly liked what had happened and kept the newspaper cuttings in her handbag as a constant reminder. She gloated over the disgusting picture of Nils in his ridiculous outfit, half-undressed and with her shoes on; she could never get over it. She did not give the presents to the children. It would be too indecent after all they had suffered from the scandal.

Tor, simply revolted, felt ashamed at being involved and thought that the least Nils could have done was kill himself properly. The money they should have received nagged at him. However little, it would have come in handy.

She looked and certainly felt older, everyone said so, she knew it for a fact. There was nothing more to live for. She did all her housework automatically these days and cooked the usual meals without joy and just wished to sink away in sleep, where she lived her own life. The only reason for continuing was that world she created at night because there they met again and everything was as before, a landscape filled with shadows where only he and she were real, and there they talked and talked endlessly, although she never remembered what about.

Four

' "Such happiness whenever it is known is to be pitied for tis surely blind." Yes, but my happiness isn't blind. That is the achievement, I was thinking between 3 and 4 this morning, of my 55 years. I lay awake, so calm, so content, as if I'd stepped off the whirling world into a deep blue quiet space and there open-eyed existed, beyond harm; armed against all that can happen.'

Virginia Woolf, *A Writer's Diary,* 9 April 1937

'26 Jan 1920. I am 38. Well, I've no doubt I'm a great deal happier than I was at 28, and happier today than I was yesterday, having this afternoon arrived at some idea of a new form for a new novel.'

Virginia Woolf, *A Writer's Diary*

24 May 1973. I am forty eight, and I have no doubt at all that I'm happier than I was at thirty eight or even twenty eight and certainly happier than yesterday, having this morning read a sentence that made sense of some words I was writing.

'It is of course impossible to free oneself from one's childhood without devoting a great deal of work to it, not only intellectually, but in re-experiencing it.'

Carl Gustav Jung

There was a curious soul twin-birth on 24 May 1925, of which I did not become aware until fairly late in middle life. All of a sudden I had to accept this coeval. She kept pushing her life on to me, so in order to get rid of her I at first started a little hurried scribbling, then penned down my dreams. Nothing made sense. I just thought I had made her up, but she insisted that this was not so — and who was I to argue? I have a somewhat mercurial mind and have in my life gone through several transmutations. I thought her another fantasy or an obstinate dream-person who had become fixed to my retina, but she insisted she was as real as myself, in many ways a replica. But being first-born, she had a few advantages and we were different, yes, but on the other hand not at all. She was I; I she. I tried to argue about our fundamental backgrounds, but she always countered with such similarities that I had to capitulate in the end.

I   In Statu Pupillari

1.   Chaos melancholia

There were landscapes, people, happenings. For instance, I came from the kind of country that seemed harmless and was sleep-inducing, where the waters were only slightly rippled and reeds swished ever so gently, where there was always a silvery black-and-white birch wood on the horizon. She came from where cliffs were rugged and waves cut into land and rock, where pine needles lay deep on the ground and under the dark crowns of trees the light was eerie and always on the move.

As for people, whereas mine were doughy and indecisive and given to futile day-dreams, hers were strong-faced, high-cheekboned and full of energies. The only thing they seemed to share was a certain harsh bitterness about their past. Their nights were filled with ghosts and their days miserably poor. Mine was gentle poverty in comparison.

She refused to leave me until she was written down and had lived herself out in me. Another person within seemed to understand what was happening and was somehow able to convey her life to me.

The people with whom Stella and her parents lived when she was about eight and when I have the first recollections of her, hid in the deepest of pine forests up north, by an angry, grumbling river. It had such force and vitality and she was secretly afraid of it, foaming in fury at anything that obstructed it, like the timber which Hjalmar, her father, worked that season. It was a highly skilled job manœuvring the thick trunks chained together that piled high on top of each other at times, and then she would see him jump on loose, floating timber to reach them. Water moving angrily all round him, he needed every bit of his agility and intelligence as much to fight and gain the upper hand as to disentangle the mass which by the second became more and more intricate and obstinate.

Stella, sitting safely on the bank, did not dare to blink in case she missed one of his moves. He was sure-footed and of ice-cold calculation, always in the end gaining complete mastery of the timber which came apart but with so many twists and turns as if in great pain, chains snapping — and then with the magic touch of his hook the muddle turned into docile trees again, floating gently down to the calmer part of the river as if nothing at all had happened. Yet they certainly could have killed him, had he been less cool and crafty.

The fears she had felt were still a tight hard knot in the middle of her stomach, more precisely somewhere just above her navel. She had a sick sensation with the relief and a sharp little pain in her head.

They thought her a strange small grown-up girl, never wanting to play with other children, preferring her own company and Hjalmar's. She seemed to have an old, wise face and people were made to feel uncomfortable by her speech and penetrating eyes. She really was only interested in Hjalmar and knew him so well and could sense how his mind worked and how it could change as the shifting summer clouds did; and when the sombre Nordic mood hit him she felt as lonely and troubled as he. Her mother Lora lived in a totally different world from them both and Stella did not feel at all connected with her; she never shared any of their moods, but had plenty of bitter comment on their behaviour.

Mother was frightened of everything, and this she hated. But then from time to time, in spite of herself, she would catch some of those despised little fears, be stupidly affected by spiders, snakes, mice, thunderstorms and the long black nights which, if he wasn't there, seemed to stretch endlessly. Then she would feel lonely and small and lived somewhere deep down in her stomach, which made her strangely nervous.

At that time she spent all day in her own company by the river so as not to lose touch with him. And when he was away in the woods she played the imagining game—she shut her eyes, tried to penetrate the darkness, and she would get the sudden glimmer of his eye, the smoke coming from his mouth or the frost in his curly beard, but they were visions that quickly vanished and she would find herself facing a blank wall again.

Lora could never understand that she always knew when he was due back home: she merely did; and there was no way of explaining it to her mother because she was too stupid to know about such matters which could not in any case be explained.

He would throw her high into the air until she almost felt she had wings, hug her until she was breathless, then be so gentle with caresses so soft for such a big man, and then they would laugh and laugh and she knew then that he loved her.

My grandfather's name was Hjalmar—was that a coincidence? I loved him too, but it was—wasn't it?—a different kind of love. He was very tall and had the bluest eyes I have ever seen and the kindest. We had a spiritual attachment; there were uncanny totally inexplicable events at the time of his death. So strongly did he come over that even other people saw him and could describe him in the utmost detail.

But to go back in time: at the age of six I had just come home from Australia with my mother. I was, it seemed, a normal, chubby, uninteresting little girl with no particular talents. I lived in a country which I would not perhaps have chosen of my own free will; both Stella and I were Swedish by birth. I had been placed geographically somewhere near the lion's heart, that is to say in the lower middle area on the map, by the shores of a long, sweet-water lake. She was living by the lean ribs of the beast, where the Arctic Circle draws a line across the map and the deep water is always cold and salty. It was a boring industrial town I had been given, a real life-killer. Most of the people seemed as grey as the buildings.

One of the many houses in which I lived had a smelly, junky back-yard full of dirt but also of mysteries; I thought it huge. There was a large metal factory behind the wall for ever churning and forging, and at the very bottom of the yard was this heap which grew curiously every day. The strange thing was that I never saw anyone put anything on it; it just grew. There were long metal rods curling and twisting into one another, shining hard shapes, odd objects with sharp edges, rusty sheets that rattled almost like thunder when you shook them—which the boys did to frighten me.

They had decided to gang up on me from the start. When not showing their teeny pricks or telling me dirty words to add to my scanty vocabulary, they were displaying how far their streams of piss would reach. There were a few variations on these games and they happened almost every day and always in the vicinity of the heap. It seemed appropriate to me even at that time.

The heap was sheltered by some very old and spreading lilac bushes which never seemed to bloom. The suckers running across the ground took all the strength from the mother tree. Then there was a row of crumbling wooden outhouses which stood like so many sentry-boxes on the alert, a barrier between the courtyard and the street outside. The boys would lure me on some silly pretext close to the toilets and then, if I didn't do as they said, knock me about, soft and hard at the same time, pushing me up against a wall, pressing themselves against me as if for protection, practising their forbidden words on me. They frightened me, but there seemed no way of escape; there were so many against me and I was the only girl. And it usually ended with my crying and their running away. I always avoided going to that toilet later and would crouch in the bushes like an animal.

The badly built outhouses looked as though they would collapse in the next storm, so loosely were they put together, and I hated the musty smell and the mound of excreta that grew monstrously and was never taken away. I had fantasies of falling into one of the holes and never being able to climb out and I loathed the buzz of the bluebottles and the rustling of the newspapers down below—I had been told of snakes living among them. Then there was my fear of the boys who always seemed to hang around the place, tapping on the slats, trying to peep through holes. I detested them with a small, cold fear in the pit of my stomach. And even today the smell of the factory is so vivid in my memory, a rusty, penetrating, acrid smell that lingered in my clothes and even inside the rooms.

I had short almost albino-blond hair with a fringe that touched my eyelashes, I had freckles and hairy arms and I was chubby. Grandfather had given me a tame crow which he had found one morning on the heap and this bird used to spend a lot of its time sitting on my head picking imaginary lice. There were no toys that I can remember, but I made shops with leaves and grasses, or built farms, the cows being constructed of cones and matches. I suppose I was quite lonely, but not much aware of it. My body functioned well; my mind was shut off.

I used to be allowed to lie between grandfather and grandmother in the early morning. The wooden bed, which was uncomfortably hard, creaked, and was converted into an upright sofa during the day. It stood in the kitchen and was painted pale blue. I was fascinated by their body smells, which were slightly sweet, reminding me of rotting apples. While grandmother, whom I didn't much like, got up to make some coffee, I would snuggle closer to grandfather to discover some of the secrets which I knew he was hiding underneath the night-shirt of soft wool he always wore. He was loving and gentle and liked having me there. I enjoyed his early morning beard of stubbly white growth and used to rub my cheeks

against it until they became rosy pink and a bit sore. It felt good,
even exciting in a way I didn't quite understand. I would try
to put my hand underneath his shirt for warmth and to get
closer and lick his arm like a puppy. Then I would try my own
dumpy arms in comparison. They were so different.

Sometimes I caught glimpses on washing night that frightened and at the same time fascinated me. On Saturday the
kitchen was full of pots and pans and steaming kettles, bowls
for the footbaths and a slightly larger vessel where you stood
to rub yourself down. I never liked looking at my grandmother
when she washed; I remember thinking how ugly she was with
her sagging breasts and skinny, dried-up body, and she had a
face which I avoided looking at—unfriendly, I thought, and
not a bit nice. I liked looking at him, though. He must have
been handsome for his age. Pictures of him as a young, newly
married man showed remarkable features of a very un-
Swedish kind, for he had dark curly hair and a rather aristo-
cratic nose. There was talk of an intricate bastard affair in the
family from rather grand quarters, and he really did look royal
in a way and did not fit his surroundings. And he was still good
to look at, with a mane of white hair, only the slightest of
bellies, and as tall as ever.

While I was hanging about the kitchen trying to catch sight
of things that were always so carefully hidden, as if there were
something shameful in them, Granny scolded me and finally
chased me out, saying I was too nosey and rude, that people
ought to be alone when they washed.

Later grandfather and I took little walks together, round the
church, to the pond with the swans, sat down on a bench while
he did his football coupons. I don't know what we talked about;
perhaps we never did talk. I only remember that it was good to
be in his company, that I felt secure, and I suppose I loved him.

Stella was jealous of her mother for being allowed to sleep with
Hjalmar every night in the same bed. She felt it not at all fair,
and thought for that matter that Lora did not appreciate it

enough. So from time to time she invented some little pain or fear just to be able to creep into his side of the bed. She curled up within his arms and legs and lay perfectly still, trying to become one with him: a heady feeling, somehow like melting away.

He always slept naked and was not at all ashamed of his body. She loved looking at it, feeling and memorizing, forming little pictures in her head of him just as he was then. And sensing her eyes on him, he smiled sleepily and laid a heavy hand on her head, caressing it so gently, and her heart beat faster then and she hardly dared breathe because she didn't want him to stop it ever: so she went to sleep all aching and stiff but absolutely happy with his smells which were so different from anybody else's.

He smelt of the whole forest, the river and the sky, and she thought him very clever to have caught all those smells and kept them upon him. He was like no one she had ever met, strong and physical yet at the same time such a soft dreamer of a man. He refused to settle down and conform in the way that other males around him seemed to do. Everyone thought him a bit hopeless, called him a vagabond and a rascal for not marrying Lora and giving her and Stella a proper home. Meanwhile, they wished they were as strong and single-minded, admitting what a good worker he was. For in any occupation he undertook he was always sooner or later the most skilful; but he always refused to be permanently hired, he wanted to move on to other things, new people, new grounds, which meant that they decided he could never be trusted.

Lora followed him against her will. Once quite pretty, there was now something sluttish about her, back slightly bent, eyes cast downwards as if some guilt plagued her; indeed she was ashamed of their state—they owned nothing, were nothing in the view of others. Their clothes were throw-outs from other people's plenty, their food almost always someone else's, their dwellings varied and sometimes sordid.

She had nothing to boast about, nothing to show except herself which she was little by little destroying. She spent her days idling and daydreaming, consuming piles of cheap magazines.

It was best for her to keep any kind of reality at arm's length, and while in the hold of her cheap romances there was no way of communicating with her; she became deaf and dumb, forgot about Stella, food, even Hjalmar. The stories, once digested, embittered her mind and made her want things desperately.

Stella had seen objects from other people's houses in her mother's purse, silly trinkets not worth having. She never looked at them squarely or mentioned them to anyone. At odd moments Lora played with them vacantly, caressing and admiring, and at such times she might wake up and become chatty, telling stories to Stella, cheap fantasies about lives lived by others, where they ought to be living and how, the stupidity of their present ways. And then she could hold Stella by her sudden excitement; her eyes shone as when she was drinking, her cheeks glowed and there was a pretty girl once more, a girl she so seldom let anyone see. Knowing deeply that her mother was somehow wrong about almost everything, Stella felt slightly tainted and did not like her feelings—yet after all, being her mother, how could she be so totally wrong?

Stella hated and pitied the Andersson twins; they looked sickly. Despite a healthy life in the country they reminded her of little, white, wiggly worms, so she kept out of their way except when they were all invited to the Anderssons for dinner on Saturday.

There was a chill in the air when the Anderssons were in a room together, as if the truth could not exist anywhere near them, and she was sure they never said what they felt. It was all politely unreal, nothing you could pin down, and the Andersson twins had also been brought up to be two-facedly sweet. She knew how they sniggered at her clothes and thought her dirty with her tousled hair; their own mousy hair was water-combed and parted every morning, then greased heavily to keep it down and down it stayed, but in ugly strands that made them look unnatural. They were beastly clean and unsnotty and smelt of the soft, yellow soap Mrs Andersson used for everything, and they had a simpering, soft look that put her off. No, she was

not a bit like them, and how they resented it and found ways of
letting her know.

They were always quibbling about their toys in a whimpering
way. Stella had never seen so many dolls, teddy-bears, rocking-
horses and cars. Even the local shop was bare in comparison.

That evening she was inexplicably filled with a desire to be
like other children and have what they had, and she recognized
Lora's bitterness in her own heart. There were heaps of discarded toys in boxes and corners, some half broken, some
perfectly new but thrown aside in a bad temper. Surely if she
took one of the smallest they would never miss it. She thought
of Lora's purse. If Lora could get away with it, why not try it
herself?

She selected a slightly soiled specimen lying in a dusty
corner. She had seen dolls of this kind hanging up in funfairs
looking as gay as butterflies, and she had thought them pretty
then, no more. It had a rosy, pink celluloid face with painted,
blue, staring eyes. The clothes consisted of chicken feathers
stuck round its waist to make a kind of hula skirt, held together by a golden ribbon crossed over the chest.

She started laying her plan. When the Andersson twins
started one of their inevitable quarrels—every ten minutes or
so—she would hide the object quickly in the blue voluminous
pants at which the twins had laughed so much. Now it would
be her turn to laugh. The doll could not possibly fall out since
the elastic was so tight that she always had red marks on her
legs which seemed to stay for ever. The pants ballooned out
and were far too big for her, a reject from a rather fat lady; she
could accommodate several dolls in the billowing folds.

As they started bickering over a dolly's tea-set and pulling
each other's greasy hair, she slipped the doll in and all of a
sudden she wanted to cry, but she bit her lips and swallowed
her sudden unhappiness and tried to think hard of the doll
whose cold little body she coud feel against her thigh; and as she
moved the feathers tickled her, which made it feel slightly alive.

She was filled with such mixed emotions—on the one hand

longing to be alone with her precious object, to be able to sit and stare at it, to hold it, know for certain it was really hers, on the other hand wanting to get rid of it, wishing she had never set eyes on any of those wretched toys. She could feel the doll now very hard, as if pressing itself against her, and the sharp edges were beginning to irritate her skin.

Hjalmar played on the small harmonium, the grown-ups sang, the twins grew finicky and cry-babyish. They wanted attention, they did not want to go to bed. There was a polite quarrel between the Anderssons over how to handle them, and in the meantime the twins fell asleep on the sofa, thumbs in their mouths, whimpering, after being subdued by sweets from the locked store-cupboard. Stella had been complimented on her good behaviour, and the twins had hated her more than ever.

In no circumstances could she tell her secret to Hjalmar. He seemed so happy, so full of food and warmth, and between the songs Lora was laughing in an abandoned way and was so unsteady on her feet that both men had to hold her up. She leant heavily in their arms and even wanted to have Stella near her. The gayer they all became, the sadder Stella felt. When the men went into another room to discuss work, and the twins were having nightmares, Lora patted Stella's cheek and said nice things to her, the words falling over one another, and Stella sat woodenly on a stool feeling the accursed doll all the time. It hurt her now; it had shifted position and one spot on the inside of her leg was sore from the constant rubbing. So she whispered to Lora about wanting to go to the toilet.

They tumbled out into the night, found the primitive shed behind the farmhouse which stood kneedeep in nettles, picked up the rusty key from the nail, and Stella started to cry. She was frightened of everything now. She cried silently at first, but soon the sobs welled up so loudly that Lora was worried, thought she was ill, patted her, and finally hugged her and begged her to say what was the matter. Lora was so different, so genuinely anxious, so soft that it took Stella a long time to talk; but at last she said, rigid with fear and unhappiness, 'The doll, it hurts.'

At once the sweetness left Lora, she turned madly on Stella, slapped her wherever she could, pulled her hair, screamed at the top of her harsh, ugly voice, 'Where is it, where've you hidden it?' and then found the thing crushed from all the violence. And Stella was dragged, lifted by her hair through the nettles which stung her legs, Lora hysterical, and they fell over objects strewn around the house, and she was at last pushed into the kitchen and flung at Hjalmar like a bit of rubbish just found.

Lora screamed highpitched accusations at them both. Stella would end up bad, he'd see, and it was his fault, the way they lived. The Anderssons looked faintly pleased with this new situation; they had embarrassed half-smiles on their faces, not quite daring to let them develop into full grins of satisfaction. Hjalmar turned white with anger and said nothing. The battered doll was lying unwanted by everyone on the kitchen table, staring at the ceiling. The twins, still half asleep, picking their noses, looked at her gleefully.

In their attic room he lay down beside her, gently touching her hair, her shoulders; and it was then that she began crying in earnest but without fear. He did not try to stop her, but later asked if she wanted to talk to him about it. She was surprised at her own reply. She wept for the Andersson twins, she said, they were too thin, too white. She cried for all their quarrelsome toys and she did not think they would ever be happy, however long they lived. She wept for the whole Andersson family, in fact, with their big house that no one ever visited, all their furniture always dusted but never used. She cried for the precious coffee-set in the locked cupboard, for the unused new sewing-machine, and she cried because the Anderssons never seemed to look at one another. She wept for Lora, for all the magazines which she so avidly read and could not share with anyone, for all those ill-gotten trinkets in her purse, she cried for her face that was hardly ever pretty any more, she cried for the bitter lines round her mouth. But she did not cry for Hjalmar as there seemed nothing to be sad about when she thought of him. And as he held her close they both went to sleep.

He left early for work and Lora did not turn up until late in the day and their supper was eaten in silence. Then Lora flung things around in a more than usually bad temper and Stella was put to bed early. Hjalmar tried to control Lora's temper, his voice was calm and deep, hers hysterical. So Stella learnt that her mother had slept with Anders Andersson that night and would again, why not?

They did not stay the expected time on this job; the situation prevented it. Everyone seemed in a poor temper except Hjalmar and Stella, who went their own way. They ended up working here and there, picking berries and digging up potatoes in odd places during the autumn. They slept in barns and damp bath-houses, were stung by wasps, caught colds and never stopped moving in search of work. Hjalmar grew quieter, Lora more noisy. When autumn seriously came upon them they caught a bus which took them to the furthest point above the Arctic Circle, where Hjalmar's sister Hilda lived in a primitive hut in the darkest wood that Stella had ever seen. The snow lay thick already, at the beginning of September.

I could scarcely have been further away from Stella between the ages of one and six. I lived in Adelaide, Australia. My basic memory from that period is of a gnawing, longing pain. I was restless and self-willed and full of daydreams. I seemed to spend most of my time in the little front garden, which was stuffed with sweet-smelling lilies and hedged in by blue grapes which I don't remember eating.

I had bitten a man in the arm quite hard because day after day I had seen him do it to a girl-friend on the beach and he never seemed to get enough of it. But he was not at all pleased when I did it to him, which rather surprised me. I had a small white dog whom I so smothered with love that he finally ran away and I was inconsolable. I cut my fringe into a jagged mess and while at work with my scissors I cut off the tail of a mouse in the trap. I made a tent in the garden of old mats and sat there in the heat of the day, mostly in a vague dream, sometimes with two little black twin brothers. I think we sat there for hours feeling each other and were never disturbed, so we quietly pursued our explorations and must have enjoyed them.

I believed in fairies; at least desperately wanted to do so. There were supposed to be some living in a very particular plant growing in the desert outside. I remember the texture of it even now, very succulent and soft to the touch, and also my disappointment when, having put water into it at night, I later crept out to look at it in the light of the full moon; it had become a slimy stinking mess and there were no fairies to be seen. I cried myself to sleep then, it was my first disillusionment. I was about four.

We had an old wind-up gramophone and two records, both Sousa marches, and some days I used to play them non-stop, dancing to the music. Standing in a window, draping myself in the curtains, I showed off to the boys and girls coming back from school. I wanted them to take notice of me; they hardly did. But I continued swinging the curtains and dancing on the chair I had drawn up to the window, I danced and danced. At least the donkey bread-man liked it. He used to stop for a long time and look at me.

The donkey wore a big paper hat against the sun and the man always gave me a bun and patted me on the bottom and said how well I could dance. Mother used to tell me I had the dancing sickness, whatever that meant. But that I could never be quite still except under that hot-house tent was a plain fact.

I spoke fine broad Australian and despite going to the kindergarten had no friends apart from the black twins, who loved to push their hands under my well-rounded bottom. But there was an old uncle of theirs who also wanted to do such things to me, which I found less of a compensation for my loneliness, so I stopped going to their house. The storms rattled over our tin roof and I was terrified of the thunder because Mother was. We both hid, she in a closet, I under the bed. It grew cold and sometimes I cried in fear.

In the rainy season the road outside became a pond where

lots of ducks gathered. There were long hours of doing nothing but watching things not happening from the window, with the rain falling in sheets; I thought it might go on for ever. We were supposed to send grandfather a picture of me for Christmas, so we trooped off to a photographer. I had been scrubbed clean and was allowed to wear my best dress. In my excitement I had picked far too many flowers, which I was going to present to my grandfather, and Mother was cross—I hadn't understood at all—and when at the studio I hadn't found my lovely grandfather I at first stubbornly refused to have my picture taken and had to be cajoled into sitting between my parents. I showed a very sour and disappointed face. I looked a horrible little girl.

Nobody understood why I was unhappy and nor did I. I had to have things my own way. I was obstinate, I never communicated much with anyone. I had already started to create an imaginary world, which I found more interesting than the real one, which just made me feel discontented and for much of the time miserable.

After many family disasters we left again for Sweden. I was about seven then and Stella a couple of years older.

Hjalmar found a job for the winter on the new railway they were cutting through Lapp territory. Living in this deep forest in Hilda's doll's house was strange and the days were long without him.

The house, consisting of one square room, had never been properly insulated or had electricity or water. Its only source of heat was an old, black wood-stove, a red-hot, pulsing heart in the place which was never allowed to die. Hilda believed in complete austerity, having at first been a follower of Laestadius, that most formidable, pleasure-hating figure, that consumer of souls. Afterwards she had tried almost every sect in the region and now belonged to a very select and obscure body which for the moment she held in awe.

There was only room for necessities. There was a table that

could be large or small by manœuvring the side-pieces, four
chairs, the sofa on which Hildebrand had been bedridden for a
long time, pushed out to full width, their own borrowed bed
standing in a corner and with its surround of white sheets for
privacy looking rather spooky. Here Lora spent most of her
days moping, while Stella helped Hilda make candles, clean the
floor, cut wood or undo the old man's socks so that Stella
could learn to make a pair for herself; after all, the old man
would never need them again. There was also a dog who
hardly ever went out—he was lame in one leg—and a cat who
sometimes came and asked for refuge.

The only reading was from the Bible, the only light two
kerosene lamps and a candlestick. There were no ornaments,
never a branch or a flower, no curtains, no mats. All was
scrubbed grey, bare and lifeless. Yet when the candle burnt
with its large smoky flame and the light outside was dimming
and the frost making stars on the windows, it was starkly
beautiful just because everything was so simple. Then there
was always a homely smell of coffee and the big black iron pot,
which was on the stove and filled every morning with fresh
snow, made a pleasant hissing noise in the room.

There was little space left for movement. It was just as well
that Lora, the old man and the dog stayed put in their places.
Sometimes she could hear Lora cry with boredom between the
rustling of bedclothes and the turning of pages, but mostly she
seemed to sleep for hours with a light snore. She had gone into
hibernation, it appeared. The cat lying for warmth on top of the
stove would purr, the dog would whimper in his sleep, and
Hildebrand, groaning with pain, would call orders to be turned
over, then snore heavily between his fits. Apart from such noises
in the house, it was the most silent world Stella had ever known.

The snow had by now reached the window-sills and the
house had almost disappeared in the great drifts all around.
They had to shovel a fresh path from the door to the wood-
shed almost every morning. They were certainly isolated. You
had to trust your nose and recognize trees and shapes on the

horizon to find the little house in the woods. And sometimes Hjalmar had difficulty in getting back for his weekends.

Hildebrand seemed to grow worse. Now he couldn't even drink the coffee in which Hilda dipped the salted bread. He at once spat it out and vomited green matter, uttering a horrible sound, while Stella, to avoid being sick herself, sang one of the hymns she had learnt. And Lora panicked, holding her ears, shouting at him to shut up.

Hilda had been sitting up at night praying for him for over a week when one sunny, frost-bitten day there appeared a small group of the oldest people Stella had ever seen. They had somehow heard that the old man was about to die and had come to pay their last visit. They squeezed into the room and stood without a word, giving no comfort, no pity, to Hildebrand, who looked lost in the crumpled bed. As if carved out of wood they were standing, dried up by the harsh weather.

Later with the coffee they talked about him in low murmurs as if he were already dead. Nobody had thought of getting a doctor; it was taken for granted that now it was only a matter of time. Stella caught glimpses of despair in Hildebrand's eyes as he heard them talk, but having by now lost the power of speech, and as most of his limbs had ceased to obey him, he had only those eyes to signal with, and sometimes they seemed to Stella very alive. She wanted to tell the others about it, but how could she? It was so hard to explain.

But what a feast it was when Hjalmar arrived home. She climbed him like a tree, buried her face in his beard, smelt his hair until it made her feel heady. The tar of the trees was in his hands still, there was woodsmoke and snow, there was wind and sun all around him. He laughed at her, caressed her, held her at a distance, and then their eyes would meet and it was such a shock of recognition, something that touched her inner-most being, such a happy, big feeling that she did not know know how to contain it. In the evening he read aloud and sang, told stories about his work and the people. She never left him. She liked to let her lips part just a very little, then gently let them move over his furry arms. It gave her goose-pimples and made her back ache, but it was so delicious a feeling that she could do it for hours. He never seemed to mind. Perhaps he never noticed.

Sometimes there were whispered conversations between her parents to which she did not want to listen. She shut off her ears and concentrated totally on his physical presence.

A few weeks after the gathering round his bed Hildebrand grew much worse and was obviously in great pain. Delirious from time to time, he would wake up and cough and gasp for breath. Then he began to smell. Lora walked back and forth like a trapped animal, even going out into the cold to avoid the death that was so slowly coming. And that was how she met the Lapp caravan on their way to the market in town and she pleaded with them until at last they consented to take her along.

So they were alone with the corpse for almost a week. Hilda could not sleep with it because of the worsening smell that soon penetrated the whole room, so in the end they carried the light brittle body out to the woodshed and set him down on the old sleigh dressed only in his nightshirt. He looked a strange ghost but the cat jumped into his lap, purring as if he were still alive.

Hilda prayed a lot but shed no tears and kept herself as busy as usual, waiting for Hjalmar's return to give orders for the burial. Lora's disappearance seemed not to upset him; he was only slightly concerned, perhaps even slightly relieved. So at last Stella was alone with him at night. She stretched out full length beside him, she placed her head in the crook of his arm and often woke up feeling his soft eyes upon her. Later he would turn to her in his sleep and put his arms round her. She was perfectly happy.

The old people came back bringing the priest with them. He looked as much of a skeleton as the corpse in the wood-shed, which now seemed to have shrunk. The coffee was blacker and stronger than usual and on this special occasion there were sugar lumps. Before blowing and sipping the hot coffee from the saucers, they had all sucked the sugar slowly as if in pain, smacking their toothless gums over it.

Stella had never seen so many ugly people at once. A smell of camphor and stale urine oozed out of their clothes. They talked, but seemed not to communicate; they seemed so cut off from one another. When Stella started to cry silently by herself, they all thought it was because of the old man. Perhaps that was so, but she also cried for them, for their wrinkles, their bent backs, the lonely smells that enclosed them, the hopelessness, and she cried for that poor Bible which they reached for all the time, as if it could cure their ills and lead them to some sort of happy land.

I have long lost count of how many schools I attended between the ages of seven and thirteen. We never stayed long enough in one place for me to learn anything or make any friends. I walked in circles round my real self, which appeared not yet to be awake. And I still only remember loneliness and the sense of not being there, but somewhere else, in limbo. I always looked out of windows. I scribbled bad poetry on every available scrap of paper and later typed it out with one finger on an old typewriter which my father had found on a rubbish heap.

Every single word I said was a lie. It was quite unnecessary, but I insisted down to the smallest detail. I fabricated the most stupid nonsense, thus creating quite a problem for myself in keeping the fantasies sorted out. I refused to be confirmed, though it would have meant a long dress and possibly a wrist watch, I didn't bother to learn reading the time until I was sixteen, I played truant from school and never listened to any of the teachers, and I certainly had no intention of learning my psalms off by heart. Was it simply that I was bone-lazy or suffered from inertia or was backward or a slow developer? Whatever the reason, I had fine-sounding excuses for my refusal of that confirmation. The fact that the other girls thought me mad bothered me not at all; I considered them so many ninnies with nothing in their thoughts but clothes, jewellery and the party they were going to be given on the great day. I thought it immoral to rattle off the catechism without caring about the words.

Instead I started to attend church regularly with a view to discovering more about it, but I resisted the Lutheran harshness, the almost empty, cold buildings, the ugliness of the people, the declamatory style of the preachers and the dull sermons. I stopped going. I have never gone since.

Brave in some ways, I was a frightened mouse in so many others. I seemed always to be followed in the streets by dirty old men; every park I entered had its exhibitionists. I always felt pursued, scared, to the point of nightmares, walking and talking in my sleep, wetting my bed well into my ninth year. My only reading matter was cheap magazines as there seemed to be nothing else available. I know nothing of what was going on in the world. I remember vague talk of war and worried faces, but nothing changed in our lives except for the rationing of butter and confectionery, but as we had little enough of those things in normal circumstances, who cared?

I was interested in nothing, but hated many things instead, most of all school. Brilliant in feigning illness, I think I had my first lessons in acting then. Once I managed to produce spots before an exam in maths and I was whisked off in an ambulance to the isolation hospital while they fumigated the school. God knows what terrible disease they thought I had, but there was of course nothing whatever wrong with me—I was just a masterly liar, even to the point of beginning to believe my own stories. Nobody trusted me and how right they were.

I was neither pretty nor ugly, too small for my age, always to my annoyance looking a lot younger than I was. I wanted so badly to grow up fast, my life seemed so dull with the world against me, and I realized with fury in my heart that all the things I wanted to do—become a sailor and travel the world, climb mountains, go exploring—were forbidden me simply because of my sex. I felt bitterly that life had cheated me out of all the possibilities.

At one point we lived above an old cinema; the neon lights were just below our kitchen window. Since this wasn't exactly the most respectable part of town, the cinema was a fine old fleapit which I came to know well, finding my way into it through an underground labyrinth. I never remember paying, but I do remember that I loved, adored, venerated Shirley Temple.

If I could never be that adventurous person I longed to become, why at least not base my life on that dummy-faced little doll of a girl? I too had dimples in my cheeks, though that was as far as our likeness stretched. My hair could scarcely have been straighter, I had no prettiness, I was ordinary, I was disappointed every time I looked in the mirror. But so stuck was I on that famous little rich girl that after much wheedling I persuaded my mother to give me the money for a Shirley Temple perm. Poor fool, I thought it was going to change my life. For days I practised saluting and tap-dancing to myself, sweating for hours in front of a full-length mirror. But the hair would definitely do it, I decided.

The hairdresser tried to talk me out of it. Mother was horrified—and so, finally, was I. I stayed in bed for a week and refused to look at myself. That hair, which had at least had a shine and silkiness to it before, was now as crinkled as wire wool with all the life out of it, and my eyes were red from weeping. I somehow realized then, lying there in gloom and disappointment, that the rich uncle who would turn me into a princess would never come; my real father hiding somewhere in the world was not going to be that famous man who lived in a castle. Obviously I was for ever to be disappointed with my life, never pretty, never to possess those wardrobes that covered whole walls and were stuffed with new dresses. It was she who had given me the idea of possessions and made me envious and when it didn't work I started to hate her. And somehow I know that my mother shared that very kind of bitterness I had begun to feel.

From that moment I learnt that I would never get anything easily. I would have to work for it, to change in some miracu-

lous way—but how? It would be a long time before I knew.
Meanwhile I invented a trick which made me believe that
everything was possible: standing very close to the mirror
until it misted up, I looked deep inside myself and found that I
could become anyone, even beautiful, even to the extent of
falling in love with myself just a little. And in due course I
liked only that self-created world and was aloof and lonely in
the real one which held no surprises and nothing in store for
me—or so it seemed then. How wrong I was.

He made her aware of the intricate shapes the snow made by
weighing down branches of the fir trees and of how to use her
nose for breathing in the forest and keep the breath in her body
and somehow store it up and use it as a form of food. She
walked, her hand in his firm grip, perfectly happy, totally secure.

At the fair smoke was pouring out of tents and stalls and the
noise was almost deafening to someone used to living in a silent
wood. The Lapps were much in evidence—it was their market
after all—and Stella liked them. The little old wrinkled women
had their whole wardrobe on their backs, hence their strange
shape and waddling walk; they were smoking pipes and nodding
sagely and throwing her glances with their sidelong eyes.
They seemed to hold aloof with some kind of secret which they
guarded.

Snow began to fall gently and kerosene lamps were lit. Some
children had made snow grottoes and now placed flickering
candles inside them, turning them into festive castles, hot and
glowing despite their cold walls. All was bliss except the
thought of seeing Lora. Hjalmar had found that she worked in
the big hotel and she was expecting them to stay the night with
her. He seemed to put the moment off, dragging his feet,
stopping at stalls, or just standing with his eyes on the busy
scene, as if he wanted to prolong their time together.

It was difficult to tear herself away from the huge Christmas
tree in the vestibule. Every branch was decorated in red, gold
and silver, but the tree within retained its strong smell and the

bright candles dripped into slow intricate patterns. But when a man full of drink began pestering them they went in search of the kitchens.

The smell of fat as they entered seemed to stick immediately to the clothes. Every surface had a layer of grease, even the floor was slippery. She had to swallow hard as the saliva formed in her mouth at the sight of so much food. In a corner sat a very small boy, eyes running, patiently peeling onions. Above the hissing of pans and kettles orders were shouted, knives sharpened, lids clanged, heavy-laden trays dumped down. The door to the restaurant kept swinging to and fro nonstop on its un-oiled hinges and each time brought with it a waft of tobacco smoke and stale air. The waitresses carried plates piled high with half-eaten food, crumpled napkins, cigar butts floating in the grease.

Behind one such loaded tray was Lora. Her hair, usually long and straight, was now frizzed out in small waves, and her face, otherwise so white and restrained, had round, bright-pink patches on the cheeks and her blood-red lips were emphasized to the point of distortion. Stella, shocked, found it impossible to take her eyes off this hard mask of a face, which seemed to grow even harder when she caught sight of them, and though she very quickly put on an expression of concern and hugged Stella, the gesture was empty, the eyes cold.

Coming too close to those strange red lips Stella pulled away ever so slightly and Lora at once felt the resistance, made a sour face and looked at Hjalmar as if to complain, but as she was in a hurry she pushed them towards the corner of the kitchen, where the onions made their eyes smart. There was a general air of confusion and bad temper and the fat man who washed the unending piles of dishes broke a glass or cup from time to time as if on purpose. Around his feet lay piles of broken crockery which he trampled with every sign of pleasure and defiance. The little boy looked up once, his eyes vacant and red-rimmed; then with a heavy sigh he returned to the never-diminishing heap.

There was a certain rhythm in the place that never let up for a moment, punctuated by the swinging doors which presented new smells, new sounds, the tail-end of a note from an accordion, a high drunken laugh; then, nearer, the sizzling of butter in a pan, the sound of running feet as someone put out the fat that had caught fire on the enormous black stove which stood red-hot and commanding in the midst of the activity.

No one talked to them or looked their way and nothing seemed to change in the kitchen. The cooks and waiters worked in this fatty world as if totally cut off from themselves.

Later Stella huddled up in the window of Lora's attic room, trying to make herself as small as possible, trying not to listen to Lora's voice, the voice she used to Hjalmar, the voice that twisted her face. She could see his reaction without looking at him, his whole body tight, his face sad. That shrill voice was a warning signal for Stella to keep away and she did so, thinking of other things.

They came in without knocking, taking their welcome for granted. They were drunk and noisy and they brought stale kitchen odours into the room. Stella recognized them at once. There was the angriest of the cooks, for whom they all seemed to have a great deal of respect, or was it fear? His name was Harald and he uttered a continuous flow of sentences needing no answers; when Harald spoke no one else said a word. He reminded her of a sick eagle, slightly moulting, which had once been a cruel and proud hunting bird but had now turned soft and mushy. Lora was shrill no more, but cooed and pirouetted in front of him as she uncorked the bottle of sweet punch and polished glasses.

The waiter and waitress Stella also recognized at once. They had made such a comic pair running in and out of the swing doors. She had wanted to laugh at his busy, angry air and in particular at his walk; his feet turned out so much that they seemed to want nothing to do with each other as they loudly half-ran over the floors. And now he was active from the start with the little plump waitress who never stopped giggling.

She was wearing a black satin dress that displayed every curve of her body, which he kept fingering as he sat beside her on the bed, sweating as much as he had in the kitchen. Meanwhile, Hjalmar sat with Stella in the alcove by the window, sipping his glass slowly and holding himself aloof. From time to time they threw a few words in his direction but never waited for his answers.

Lora, her eyes large and glistening, head on one side, was nodding agreement to everything Harald said as she bent her body towards him, swaying closer all the time. At one point the laughter, which Stella could not understand, reached such a pitch that Lora was leaning against Harald helpless and shaking, the waitress sat crying with laughter on the waiter's knee as he lay back on the bed kneading her bottom with his hands. When Hjalmar suggested quietly that as the bottle was now empty they might all go to bed, the room seemed to fall apart, the waitress rolled over on the bed, bent double as if in pain, and the waiter followed suit, and at that moment the black satin seemed to split, because there was now a large white breast bobbing out of it. The waiter at once grabbed it with hungry fingers while digging into her neckline for the other, which he soon hauled out of its darkness. He snorted piggishly and the laughter rose again. Lora kept stroking her hips as if in agony until Harald clamped her hands tight over her belly and started stroking her until she was absolutely still, her face a mask of silent laughter.

Seeing Hjalmar move closer, sensing his anger, Harald quickly said there was a bottle in his room, they would go and finish it there. The waitress, now naked to the waist, half fell out of the room with the waiter still grabbing at her body. The floorboards creaked for a long time after their departure.

She wished she was not such a cry-baby, but she tried to be as quiet as she could, not wanting him to see her tears. He put her on the bed and covered her with his coat. Her teeth were chattering with a cold that seemed to come from within. He walked back and forth while she cried for their laughter, for

Lora's red lips and her sickly perfume, she cried for the white, soft breasts, the flat feet, for Lora's gestures and her harsh voice, cried for the eagle that had gone bad, she cried for the whole hotel with its smelly kitchen and slippery floor, for the piles of dishes and the little boy's red-rimmed eyes and those greasy plates. She cried inwardly and was shaking with cold.

Hjalmar tried to still her, holding her in his arms, and finally so laid the whole weight of his body on her as to give her comfort, and thus had they gone to sleep.

It was still dark when they left. They walked down sleeping corridors with shoes waiting outside doors, polished and patient. The hall stood large and desolate and had a strange burnt smell. When Hjalmar lit a match to help them find their way they saw the devastation. The glittering tree was wrecked, all colours gone, a burnt-down skeleton of a tree. There was water all over the floor and buckets all round it.

They hurriedly left the sad sight and were soon tramping on an ice-cold road which made her toes go numb. A half moon showed them the way. There was no sound but the painful shriek of the snow as they walked. Hjalmar carried her on his back and she went to sleep again. He was no eagle gone wrong. He was everything that was beautiful, a dewy spider's web catching the early sun, the intricate veins of a newborn leaf held against the light, a piece of coloured glass washed smooth by an angry sea, he was all that and much much more.

In the woods she walked again, hands tucked in his. They said nothing; they listened to the woods, their thoughts. He stopped to light a pipe and warm her hands round it, and on his knees in front of her looked at her hard and steadily, and at once she was in his arms, he was hugging and kissing her hands, cheeks, hair, mouth, and she responded so eagerly that, taken aback, he laughed and laughed at her. So once more she slipped her hand in his and they continued to tramp homewards.

I was slothful, inert, untrustworthy, joyless, insecure, vacant, indifferent, dishonest, aloof, suspicious, apathetic, unhopeful.

Sometimes I felt like a little old woman walking empty-eyed and crippled. The days seemed permanently overcast. I lost so many precious years in this sloth. I felt comfortless because I knew there was no one there to give me any comfort even if I had asked for it. It seemed that no one cared for anyone.

The days dragged. Saturday nights were spent reading cheap magazines while my parents played cards. Boredom would make me fall asleep at last, to be woken up in the middle of the cold night for the walk home, disgruntled, frozen, eyes fixed on my feet. I knew that life had nothing in store for me, and in bed a heaviness enveloped my body. We continued to move, small towns, the big city, the country for a spell, then back again to different parts of the city. Holidays were bicycle trips to my grandparents, dusty roads, endless pine forests. There was no joy in it. Once there, I would try to steal as much as I could from my grandmother's purse, and the coinage taken was never enough to be noticed. I never liked her.

I was in a state of pitiable ignorance about all matters, including sex which no one had explained to me. Things like periods were never mentioned and I was deeply scared when they first came, and did not dare tell anyone for days. I was given a sanitary towel crocheted by hand. I hated it and felt ashamed. There was no reason why one should have this damned thing happen; it was to be accepted.

My grandparents had rented a small house, with a lodger, next to an outdoor café and, though I longed to be in it, I suppose we couldn't or wouldn't afford it. There was a small orchestra scraping away behind our hedge of lilac. It made me dream and soften within. There was the constant natter of knives and forks — what delicious things could they be eating? — how I envied them. But what I never envied were the tight-mouthed, skinny women with hair done in tight knots. They assembled on the other side of the street. There was the non-conformist church in which they sang and prayed for hours, when I and several other children used to creep to the frosted windows, trying to peep down into the swaying, screaming mess of bodies shouting for their god. And did I or did I not see odd events taking place there which excited me? Certainly there were terrible rumours which we discussed endlessly and we never let an opportunity to peep pass.

Nothing was good, nor was it, I suppose, bad either. I had no idea of how to escape that monstrous self-pity in which I seemed to be wading. I had a talent for making myself more isolated than need be. On a camping holiday we were several times flooded out of our tent. The Philadelphia was there in full force with a fine baritone well-loved by everyone, always with a circle of young admirers round him. I remember vividly how he sat in front of a dish of bananas and whipped cream, laughing and spooning it out to the children, while I stood outside the group, also wanting to taste, greedy but not wanting to admit it, and he beckoned to me to come and have some too. But I ran away, finding the moment disgusting; I felt he was buying them.

Yes, things around me were not what they should be, I sensed. Relationships were wrong in their bitterness, anger, much hate, the wrong people tied to each other for life, morbidly destroying themselves, and yet I felt no strength within and no blood. And why was I a brownie for a while? Certainly I was no good at learning my credo, doing knots or praying, but I could manage the theatricals so well that it went a bit to my head and I joined a children's amateur group, only to become jealous of the daughter of the leader who of course always got the big parts and who was posh. And I really detested two girls who went to the opera school in the hope of becoming ballerinas.

If they could walk on their toes, so could I. I demonstrated it. They were so astonished they gave me their discarded shoes and for the next few months I practised for hours until my toes were a bleeding mess. But I did dance at the next soirée (anything could be done if one wanted it enough) to the 'Blue Danube' played on the gramophone; my knees were horribly bent, but I *was* on my toes. I remember crying with pain afterwards.

I carried the coffin with five other girls at a brownie funeral, tears streaming, but then with a different pain. She had been my first friend ever. There was a party afterwards, and when the cake with the big black cross was cut, I was sick. I left the brownies and learnt popular songs like 'Night and Day' from a record and sang them at get-togethers — unsuccessfully, as they always seemed to play the piano in the wrong key on purpose. They had to have someone to laugh at, I thought, and apparently I had copied the words out wrongly. I heard the tittering, and I cried then too in the vestibule among the clothes.

But, keeping pretences up all the time, I walked round with a book of psalms and said I sang at serious concerts. The lying was really brilliant. Once I completely fooled a group of schoolmates into believing I had gone blind, I kept it up for an hour, then laughed; they never forgave me. I tried to sneak into parties to which I hadn't been invited and felt miserable. I liked one teacher in one of my many schools and, after for so long being the worst in class, I was suddenly for one term at the top. But I stole and borrowed, copied, cheated myself to my new position, since I dared not trust myself. At the exam was hung one painting which I had done during that glorious term, of a princess locked in the tower of a castle, a dragon circling its foundations and spitting fire. It's the perfect picture of me, locked within myself, my own worst enemy, at once the princess and the dragon.

Everyone was cheating and it was taken for granted. Many things seemed to have fallen off lorries. Owners of factories, shops, businesses, were always so much exploited by their employees that I myself caught the habit of giving the rich bastards one in the nose. There was so much hatred under the petty thefts, so much a sense that we would never be able to crawl out from under our stones and sit in the sun with the lucky ones. We would never even win prizes in the tombola. Only the rich did. So we gave them all the dirt we could and revelled in our ignorance of things.

A nasty little affair occurred when I once went to a summer camp for a week. A titled girl had her birthday there and Mum came, fat and bejewelled from another world, with cream and strawberries for us all. The daughter herself, quite dumpy, always over-ate, but that day she could not finish her strawberries for the excitement. I never liked her; she talked and behaved differently. That night I was in the washing-up team and initiated the polishing-off of the left-over strawberries. We shared them; we giggled; and thought nothing of the consequences.

Next morning everyone owned up except me. I denied that I had eaten any and blamed it on the others, who were listening outside the door when the leader interrogated me. They said I was bad. In my heart I agreed with them; I neither liked nor respected myself. I was lonelier than ever.

It was a colony of tents on a wooded hill by a lake, infested with ticks and mosquitoes. There was a stonepit with the juiciest of raspberries, but it also housed vipers which I had seen coupling in the midday sun; there seemed to be hundreds of them coiling and hissing, reminding me of the activity in the camp. In all those blue, green, red, impermanent little canvas dwellings similar things were happening, what was the difference?

The police often turned up. There was always trouble of some kind, brawls, drunks, stolen goods, wrecked tents, whining girls—a squalid place that held one like a magnet, with one common denominator: boredom. For it somehow seemed to be better where others were equally bored. There was a horrid consolation in it. Bluebottles and wasps hovered round the overfilled wastebins. One's feet were caught in sticky sweet-papers. There was the usual kiosk with the usual bitter-faced lady who had seen all yet nothing.

It is difficult to eradicate that half-rotten smell of fruit, the chocolate melting, the bad ice-cream. I am sure that the showers were never cleaned, they were always full of hair and grit; you caught foot-rot there. Nor was the water in the lake that clean; the used rubbers floated. On the shore a drunk man

I

had fallen asleep in the noon heat and his brain had melted, a young boy had dived from a rock and split his skull, a young couple had committed suicide badly and their screams of pain agonized the memory for weeks afterwards. These were everyday happenings. The place should have been marked on the map as an evil spot; instead we all flocked there.

It was never really hot that summer or cold, but clammy; the mind became sticky and fatigued. People who played cards in the bushes ended up quarrelling. Clothes were strewn about. Towels hung sour and wet between the tents. There was so much paraphernalia: pots and pans, half-eaten potatoes, enamel washbasins with a ring of dirt and grey water at the bottom, a soggy piece of soap floating in a plate, boxes and papers, bottles and flies everywhere.

Saturday nights were frightening in the number of drunks moving in the shadows ready to pounce. There had been a murder case; one man was suspected. We kept bad friends and kept them secret, smoked in doorways, put make-up on crudely, behaved noisily, ogled boys. To know their secrets. To be loved. In love. To be totally immersed in love. All longing, ambition, need, was for love, perhaps because of the loveless world all around. Those we picked up, those crude, empty-faced boys so full of themselves, could not possibly have been anybody's darlings.

He was dull but tough, a bad sketch drawn by the Almighty, but hard in body as the sun struck the green canvas. The heat inside was intense. Outside the boys were quiet, not wanting to miss anything. But everyone missed the penetration. There was disappointment. Through the knotted-up tent eyes were peering, bright as lizards but with drooping lids — 'She's bleeding.' But there were only a few sickly drops. Bicycling home, rigid with loneliness. She too. Stella. We nearly had an accident in the tramline. Got caught on the curve, a tram coming fast downhill, wildly clanging the bell. Wanted that accident. Why not? But then the brain snapped at the very last moment. We worked ferociously to get out, and we did.

'I am 48 ... I am stuck fast in that book — I mean, glued to it, like a fly on gummed paper. Sometimes I am out of touch but go on; then again feel that I have at last by violent measures — like breathing through gorse — set my hands on something central. Perhaps I can now say something quite straight out; and at length; and need not be always casting a line to make my book the right shape. But how to pull it together, how to comport it, press it into one. I do not know; nor can I guess the end.'

Virginia Woolf, *A Writer's Diary*, 26 January 1930

2. *Non compos mentis*

Their eyes firmly locked against the world, their shoulders rounded, their backs bent, their hands tightly clasped in their laps, the brothers were ardently in the midst of their prayers, voices harsh and uniform. Now and then one might lose contact with the group, then the voice stood outside the humming chorus like a soloist inventing a new cadenza, but almost immediately it resumed the steady monotony once more.

They seemed solemn and neurotically intense while sipping the hot coffee, clawlike fingers holding on to the saucers, crunching the sugar lumps between the few sharp teeth they still had left. Apart from their blowing the steam off the coffee with parched lips, the sucking, the swallowing, the only sound was the constant hum of the paraffin lamps and from time to time a landslide of snow from the roof, gathering momentum as it fell with a heavy thud on the ice below. Spring floods and sunbursts were a long way off. Everything was hard, sparkling, white and lonely.

The new sister arrived late with her husband Aaron. She brought a smell of polished leather, untouched reams of cloth, cough-drops, and there was a distinct reek of animals around them. They had come by horse and sleigh directly from the village store they kept. He fitted perfectly into the group, but not she, who had brought light into the room despite the black, starless night. She somehow forced them to meet her eye. To their own surprise they squeezed out a tight little laugh or two and at once felt ashamed; after all they had come on godly business. The aura that surrounded her made them ill at ease, they didn't understand it and did not altogether approve.

The little dark figures huddled back into the shadows, except for the sister who spread herself by the lamp, was illuminated by it, her cheeks rosy, face shining, eyes shut; she was almost blinding in contrast to the crumpled cut-out figures who had begun their orisons.

Behind the white sheet Stella was cosy and private. The opening flapped in brief gusts of wind, so the scene unfolded itself intermittently; smoking candles and flickering lamp made the ceiling dance, sounds of the prayers were soporific. Hjalmar's nightshirt, stuffed under the pillow, was good to hold on to. He would come back at the weekend, lie in the same bed, be loving and warm; it was easy to dream about him and she was hoping to do exactly that when a foreign note, metallic, struck the ceiling. Though at once hushed down by the others, it seemed to gather force and rise and move away from the murmurs.

It came from the new sister, now with eyes wide open and startled, and one after the other they shut their frightened eyes tightly at what they had seen and, raising their murmurous voices, tried to drag her back. Battle commenced; but her voice was bewitched, rising like a lark, soon lifting the roof, soaring, fluttering wings against the falling snow. She would not accept their grey language. She was glorifying, she was worshipping. 'Let us all give praise to the Lord's name, praise him sun and moon and every single star that shines, for you are the God and good of us all.' She was transported far away and trembling gently; no matter how hard they tried to bring her back, she was irretrievable, her body swaying with the words.

Against their will they forced themselves to look again and there was real fear in their eyes. 'O Lord God of truth, O fountain of mercy and joy, you are the eternal truth.' There was panic in the air and the murmurs stopped as if at an order. She was alone at last, singing.

Aaron got up, awkwardly moved across to her as if not quite knowing what to do, took a deep breath and slapped her hard on both cheeks. They all sat still and expectant. They might forgive her if she stopped now. She was swaying dangerously on the chair, her voice pierced the room. 'O dearest love, how long I have waited for you. I was asleep and you awakened me. I want to lift my heart up to you so that you should see my love shine like a sun, a flower in the snow, thanks be to God.'

The sheet in front of the bed trembled, but it wasn't God who came to Stella's mind. It was Hjalmar. Her body quivered, her flesh sprang into goose-pimples: yes, to shine like a sun for him, to show him all the love that lay within her seemed impossible. The glorifying voice made everything stand still. She stared at the sister who was now in a deep trance, tears streaming down her face. 'O my true life, my God, O lovely light, I hunger and thirst for you.'

Stella was aware of a tingling sensation in her stomach. Her mouth was parched. Why wasn't he there, his body relaxed and breathing gently beside her, fingers touching her hair? Hands caressing. 'You touched me and I burst aflame, great are your ways.'

They were whispering excitedly among themselves. One brother, tearing himself away from the group, fell into the sister's circle of light and tried to follow her ecstasy. His voice was thin. 'Yes, O lord, we praise your name.' He touched her hands, her knees, as if for comfort and strength, as if to be besmirched by her frenzy, but they dragged him back into their dark circle again and argued in harsh, hushed voices. Her loneliness was supreme. 'O my God, restore me and smile upon me and I shall find peace. Pity the sinner who sings your praises.'

Aaron had gone to the darkest corner and turned his stony face to the wall, his hands and body in a position of prayer. His nose sniffled, his throat whimpered. There was a scuffle between two of the brothers, broken sentences, angular movements, then suddenly the meekest and skinniest of them all took charge, twisted with a boyish grin the sister's arm behind her back. Her voice rang louder. 'O Lord, give me wings to fly to your heaven.'

Hilda had stared at the sister at first in horror, then in fascination, and now there was a sharp glint in her eye and two feverish spots on her cheekbones as she swayed in rhythm with the sister's cadenzas. The whole room was on the move. Even the white sheet round the bed seemed to be alive, bulging like a sail in a frisky breeze. Stella heard herself whimpering with not exactly pain, yet pain it was, unease filling the body with a sense of being totally paralysed; yet her eyes were wide open and saw through the chink what was happening now. Hilda was slapping the sister's face, mildly at first; then harder and faster came the slaps, her hair had fallen and mysteriously her wrinkles seemed to have vanished, she had found a different and younger face. The brother who had been first to break away towards the sister was back in a kneeling position, holding tightly her fat legs, his face twisted and mesmerized. 'O love ever burning, set me on fire.'

The cat crouched on the floor, hairs on its back bristling, tail enormous, eyes large and uncomprehending. The sheet hung slack in front of Stella as she heard but did not see the sister's ode that soared on, further and further from the ground, and the falling laments of the others were painful to the ears.

Next time the sheet opened up a view — it seemed an eternity — there were changes. The brother had crept up to the sister on his knees and, in an attempt to stop the flood of words, was kissing her passionately and hard. 'My bridegroom.' Hilda and another sister were holding her face, pulling her hair tight. The meek brother was still wrenching her arm behind her with the expression of a dying man, a fish gasping. From the slobbery kisses saliva ran down the sister's cheeks, mingling with her tears; hands, grabbing at her enormous breasts, ripped the material and laid them bare and white above her belly, then fumbled downwards, dragging the dress above her knees, revealing wool, pink corsets, suspenders. It was a fight to reach the body but there it now was, a soft area of flesh whiter than the sheet that was flapping dangerously out. They all stared in awe at the red mound of curly hair, as if it were aflame, and in a moment he lay drooling in that fire, while with the other hand he opened his trousers and pulled himself more and more erect. 'The water I drink is your blood, beloved, the bread I taste your body.'

Another sister lay crumpled on the floor, tearing at her clothes, rolling like a boat on the waves. Stella felt herself moving, her body was hurting her now; she pressed Hjalmar's nightshirt against her belly as the only comfort, and she wanted to cry out to them to stop but did not dare. The sister had opened her legs wide, her body shifting in a curious rhythm that made them all wail in unison. Hilda was rubbing herself against a sister, the chair, even against the meek brother who was groping in the air for comfort. 'When I am with you and you listen to me there will be no more sorrow, for my life will be wholly filled with you.' She screamed out the last words and parted her legs even wider. The brother, also screaming, fell upon the other sister who began rocking him into a frenzy.

It was surely the moment for the room to burst into flames, the house to fall apart. But it stood, walls intact, as grey as ever, and Stella could not believe it. She herself was quivering, wet, exhausted and frightened, lying as still as possible, hardly daring to breathe. 'Have pity on me, O Lord, in my misery.' The sister's voice was as strong as ever. 'I am a poor sinner, yet I praise your name.' The others seemed to be spent, yet they started hitting her again, harder now, working themselves up to anger. 'O Lord, my God, look upon me and listen to me, open the door for me.' And at last someone thought of stuffing a red handkerchief down her throat. 'O Lord, my hope, my saviour ...'

A dreadful silence followed. Clothes rustled. There were

embarrassed coughs. The sister's face bulged red, her eyes fading, but now they seemed to have forgotten her in their busy efforts with themselves, their boots, shawls, mufflers, and finally it was Aaron who tried to put her together again with a fumbling hand: the head limp, falling, a rag doll, a broken flower.

Stella heard them slapping her outside in the snow, but there was no other sound except that of the sleigh and horse departing. The house seemed no longer to belong to Hilda. She walked in, eyes far away, did none of her usual duties but sat down heavily at the table, fell asleep and snored loudly. It was icy cold. The stove was almost out. Lights flickered. But if they died of cold now, Stella thought, did it really matter? Life could surely never be the same again. But then somehow Hjalmar was there within her, whispering her name, and the fire was soon revived, a new candle burning brightly, the place in order again. She swallowed the salt tears as they quietly flowed. Everything hurt, but she could not cry properly. She had to try to bury this night somewhere, but at the moment it stood crudely alive on the screen of her memory. She did not dare shut her eyes, so did not sleep at all.

A titled, weak-faced young man used to bring small valuable trinkets to the pawnbroker's shop where I worked for a short time. At least once a week he parked his smart sports car outside, almost ran into the shop and out of his pockets fished snuff-boxes, silver spoons, old coins. And as if he scorned the money he received in exchange, he stuffed it loosely into his pocket, looking no one in the eye, and tore off again. He never reclaimed his property, but always brought more — though only objects he could stow about his person.

One day with the delicate salt-cellars he flung a visiting-card on the counter. It was an impressive title. If I had a boring moment, why not call him? He could liven things up. The insolent eyes looked at me briefly; the arrogance of birth and money was there. Had I seen the picture in the paper from the hunt ball? It was good publicity for him. He was going to be an actor. Duly impressed, I thought about my life in which almost every moment dragged with a boredom that made me feel juiceless, a sucked-out orange.

On our way to the party at his parents' home—they were away—he talked big. Every passing was a risk, but what was the point of a sports car if you didn't travel fast. The tyres screeched. His mind was unconnected. He would have made the eagles scream with his arrogance.

The house had known palmy days. Prejudice, class-consciousness seemed to be built into its very walls. It was solemn, stuffy and elegant. Everyone showed contempt for it by soon vomiting over the velvet chairs and Persian carpets after pouring down quantities of drink. The girls had turned up their noses and laughed when I was brought in and went on behaving like window-dressing until they got sozzled; you could see their well-bred manners go with each empty glass. Shamelessly they went for the boys' trousers like animals pouncing, opening their mouths and anuses without discrimination. It was soon bedlam. Into a corner, mouselike, sober and intimidated, I had crept. I was horrified by the speed and ugliness of events.

I was expected to join in. I shook my head and cringed further into my corner until finally I couldn't speak at all. My host then took me up to the parental bedroom. He had thought me a virgin at least, but—he feebly shouted—these working-class whores started early. He was bored and in any case couldn't make it and took a revolver from a drawer and aimed at the window. The glass shattered.

Uniforms from a former war were now hauled out of boxes. Rusty medals hung from the moth-eaten cloth. The gun-room was ransacked for muskets and rifles, sporting guns, fencing equipment. African spears were unhooked from the walls. The place had to be turned into a battleground.

I stood unarmed, trying desperately to be neutral, making myself small, but I was the one-piece resistance movement and had to be caught and destroyed for not playing their game, for not being one of them; they felt a consuming scorn for me and my like. With heart beating I was chased up and down stairs, along corridors, spears tickling my back. I was afraid there would be bullets in one of the guns they kept triggering away behind me. The girls laughed wildly as I raced for the third or fourth time through the big room where they lay in their own vomit, egging on the boys who cornered me and flicked at me with their fencing swords. They had found the perfect scapegoat.

They pushed me to my feet and again starting chasing me up and down the house. Out of the corner of my eye I had glimpsed a balcony and with renewed energy I dashed towards it. But there was no way of locking the door from outside, no time to think, and no alternative but to jump, whatever lay below, with their voices storming behind me.

Screams of anger followed the fall. A sharp pain stiffened my body and I could hear the clicking of guns above me. There was a pause. Then in the stillness of the clear blue night the shot I had been expecting rang out at uncomfortably close range. I held my breath, time halted, not a branch or leaf moved. Questions flashed through my mind. What was wrong with my life, why was I so crossed, why had I been dealt such a rotten hand?

A commotion on the balcony brought me back to reality. A fight seemed to have broken out. Another shot split the air and a long surprised scream widened the split. I belly-crawled out through the damp bushes. The earth had a rotten smell. There was smoke in the air. I did not dare to cry and my throat was dry and aching. The gorse clung to me and I fought with my hands in pain. Limping along the road towards some streetlights in an ornamental tree I heard them come. I hid in a ditch. The police cars flashed past. The villa quarter was asleep, as if dead. They felt secure behind their locks and bolts, their burglar alarms; nothing woke to the cruel noise of the sirens, not even a dog. I had no idea of time or even of where I was, but managed to get a lift from a newspaper van. I was crying at last and cried my way silently all the way into town and could find no words to explain. What could I have said? What was there to say?

'These moments of despair—I mean glacial suspense—a painted fly in a glass cage—have given way as they so often do to ecstasy.

'And off winged my mind along those wild uplands. A hint for the future. Always relieve pressure by a flight. Always violently turn the pillow: hack an outlet. Often a trifle does.'

Virginia Woolf, *A Writer's Diary*

3   *Via media*

Life changed for Stella after that night of prayer. The lonely house in the woods was full of people asking questions and Hilda was curiously quiet. Stella followed her example. What could she have said? The truth? Never. So she went with Hjalmar to his workmen's hut which lay buried in even deeper snow.

Again the inside was centred on a plump black monster of a stove, seemingly full of its own importance in bringing warmth and a glow to everything. The bunks surrounded it; everyone could see its cosy flames. Jutta, the girl in charge, was like a moon round whom the men moved in orbit; rosy, sturdy, openhearted, she treated them as babies, scolding, praising, loving, laughing. There were four men including Hjalmar, all as different as the rags in a patchwork. One small and weedy, always showing off, boasting about his conquests, highly strung, touchy; another steady, slow and kind, with evil-smelling feet, but never minding how much they teased him; and finally one who had been in trouble with the police, who cringed if the door opened unexpectedly, who always carried pictures of the family he never saw, to whom he sent money, for whom he was wearing himself out. All were at once kind to Stella, brusquely gentle, trying to make her feel at home.

Numbed by the events of that night, she had difficulty in going to sleep despite being next to Hjalmar. The bunk was narrow, so she really felt his closeness, but she was uneasy in a room full of noises. The stove crackled and squeaked, and as the wood of the hut expanded in the immense heat groans came from the walls. From time to time a branch swished over the roof, and there was a curious singsong of snores, whistles and grunts from the men. But apart from the sounds she dared not close her eyes that night for fear of seeing those dreadful images that had stuck to the inside of her brain.

She tried to concentrate on Hjalmar lying so very close and alive, lips slightly parted with a hint of a smile, hands in a position of loose, relaxed prayer. A cold wind blew through her heart. Those gentle hands clasped in that fashion made her sob inwardly, for they reminded her of hands so cruel. Silently and at last and with some relief the tears flowed and made the pillow wet.

She tried to drown the memory of those ugly, praying bodies with her tears, to kill them with every drop that fell on the naked hollow of his shoulder. He slept as peacefully as a crusader outstretched on his tomb, knowing nothing of the great lake of sadness she was in. She loved him just as much, perhaps even more, but felt somehow cheated as he lay there on his back, gently breathing.

In the hut all was routine. There were no surprises. She felt secure with the same meals, week in, week out, the same jokes, the strict hours. She grew used to the men's habits and was not at all put off by their naked bodies on washing night. Nobody seemed to think it odd that a girl of fourteen with breasts beginning to bud should walk naked among them or sit on Hjalmar's knee. They teased him about his big girl and laughed when he became erect while drying her in front of the stove. She wanted it to stay; she was proud of his powers. But Jutta slapped it down with a laugh and told him to behave. It was all friendly enough, but she was jealous when Jutta scrubbed his back with such obvious enjoyment and she felt a pang when Hjalmar kissed her afterwards full on the lips as thanks.

And there were nights when he wasn't there in bed when she woke up. Then a pain so deep and so difficult to locate would make her throat dry and her eyes smart. She knew where he was, from Jutta's small groans, the creaking bunk, the quiet giggles afterwards. He would come back hot and sweet-smelling and fall asleep like a child. But however much he felt for her in his sleep, the pain stayed and she felt alone as she never had before. Something had changed.

I kept following the evil star. Nothing could shift me to another course. I was virtually unemployable when I finished school. Teachers were relieved to see me go; they washed their hands of the impossible. I coudn't even work as a shop-assistant, because my maths was almost non-existent and in any case I hated money as I was never going to have any of it myself. The humdrum was so surely mapped out for me that I was quite prepared to accept the lowest-paid and most deadening job.

But I wasn't even taken by the shoe factory, as I didn't dare to show my school report which they had demanded. However, I got a job in textiles; the prison opened its arms to me and I served a sentence — but for what offence? I obeyed orders, sat on a wooden bench from eight to five with seven other girls, removing the tacking from men's suits. We knew we were mediocre, we had been driven into a corner, and we gave grudging service, clockworking our way in and out of the factory, being even forced to ask the foreman permission to go to the lavatory. He placed his beady fat glances on our legs, and we pushed our skirts up higher so that he could see our knickers and plump thighs. Agonize the bastard was our motto.

Supervision was strict and no talking was allowed, but as soon as the bastard had turned his back there was no stopping us, despite limits to the topics of conversation, so I sang every thing I knew from nursery ditties, hymns and school songs to those with filthy words, especially when the self-made fuhrer was on his way down with the whip between the clanging looms.

They tried to make robots of us and with some they

succeeded. The two fat women on the machine in front of us had been well and truly brainwashed. The only thing they hated as much as we was this little swine of a watchdog. A woman had given in to him once. He had taken out his wretched little prick and commanded her to suck it until he came in her mouth. She had been unable to eat anything for days afterwards. As the story went round the factory, everyone compared notes on how filthy men were.

I hated that feminine stale smell of armpits and the curse. Always there were bloody sanitary towels stuffed in corners of the toilet, where we would smoke half a fag while looking out of the high prison windows with empty eyes. In the cellar for our lunch-hour we gossiped sex again over our tin boxes of cold fry-ups. And why I never rebelled against finding myself in such slack water is just beyond me. Perhaps because I was without hope.

And in the evening I was off to the seedy dance place which lay in a rotten part of the town, furious whenever I was asked to dance by proper nice boys. I wanted the really tough ones. You could see how bad they were, how rottenly they would treat you — which was just what I almost wanted: it fitted my life. But they never came my way. They saw an undersized, mousy girl alone and never even bothered with a second glance. However whorishly I tried to make myself up, I still looked just plain. But the nice boys played their tricks too and it was no good. The circumstances were always sordid, at beer parties, on someone's filthy mattress, in some dank pissy entrance, stockings laddered, face drawn, black rings under eyes; and I would traipse back next morning to the factory, trying to be a puppet again, the tool of my trade in my hand, a sharp blade ripping away those stitches, and a blunted pen ticking off how many coats I had unpicked — yes, a moron, and feeling it, knowing it — until one day in despair, hysteria, boredom, something happened in that feeble brain and I threw that precious instrument away and walked out of the damned place, never to see it again.

K

An old-fashioned haberdashery on the other side of town took me on to dust the boxes of buttons and ribbons and to run errands. The old fat lady who owned it was certainly not kind. There was a smell of stale urine around her, so it was a relief to get out of the shop. The parcels were always small and the rather grand ladies living in large Strindbergian mansions in the smarter streets sometimes gave me a tip. Although I would usually spend it on a hot-dog or an ice-cream, I never liked this money that was handed to me so easily but always somehow with an expression of guilt.

Once a man in pyjamas opened his door and asked me to come in and wait. Then, in a doorway, he beckoned to me, taking out his thing which grew in his hands until somebody came and pushed him out of sight and there was much shouting behind shut doors. I left with the largest tip I had ever had.

Then there was the fat brother of the shop lady. Sitting down in the little room behind the shop they almost filled the available space, he with his belly on the table with the coffee cups. They were gluttons. I was always running off to the confectioner to fetch boxes of creamy cakes for them. His hobby was photography and one day I was asked to deliver a parcel of handkerchiefs to his flat. I don't know why I felt uneasy, perhaps because of his wet eyes when he looked at me and his handshake on both meeting and parting, a perspiring, soft-as-dough, overlong handshake. I stood outside the door for a long time and heard him walking about inside emitting long, loud burps.

He took his time opening the door. Again he shook my hand, this time enclosing it in both of his, and his eyes were exceedingly moist. Wouldn't I join him in a cup of coffee as I had such a long walk back and it was raining? It was all set up. A carnation with a feathery bit of greenery stood in a vase, cigarettes lay on a silver plate. The coffee stood on an ornamental Turkish table and he looked extraordinarily silly perching next to it on a small chair. I dared not smile. With the second cup he tried to tell me how pretty I was and how he really wanted to take my picture. I was embarrassed; he offered money; I gave no answer. He offered me more. Could I come after I finished work? He would have all the lamps set up, I ought to get into films, he had connections. Well, why not? I had once waited outside the film company's grand gates in the hope of being an extra and had finally been admitted to fill in a form and present a polyphoto, though nothing had ever come of it. So I said yes. He tipped me with a note when we shook hands, not looking at me. Once I had agreed, he seemed to want to get rid of me.

I hated the idea of going back and paced the street for an age. Then he was breathing heavily. There was a glass of punch inside me almost at once, then another, and he was playing a rather scratchy record. I saw no photographic equipment. He said he had a present for me, a large box of chocolates and a pair of silk stockings. I was speechless, he poured another glass, I was hot and uncomfortable. I felt just silly. He was breathing more heavily now and I was suddenly and without warning moved from my chair into a corner where there was a divan. He was on top of me before I knew it, crushing me, and I screamed as he plunged for my knickers. More and more agitated he became, then abruptly limp, so I crawled from beneath that mountain of flesh with shaking knees. Taking my coat, I didn't dare to look round. The noises were dreadful.Perhaps he was dying.

I had forgotten my purse. It was raining. I had to walk all the way home, a good hour.

I told his sister next morning and of course she didn't believe me. I must leave at once without pay. When she phoned him I could hear the dreadful grunts at the other end. We closed the shop for the day. I was asked to wait while she saw her brother and a taxi was called. I stayed that long, grey afternoon and I was frightened. On her return she avoided my eye and gave me my purse and his presents and put into my hand more money than I had ever seen and sent me away, with a last harsh word that she would call the police if I ever came back. That was easy. I never wanted to see either of them again.

It was high summer. Mother and I went fruit-picking for a month to escape from town, in a small wooden house where everything could be heard through the walls. Upstairs the son of the proprietor lived and a farm-girl slept with him every night, thumps and bed-springs endlessly; and there were groans from next door where two middle-aged lady pickers were up to something that always seemed to continue until I fell asleep.

The white heat outside went on day after day. We were stung by angry wasps among the raspberry canes; they were as restless as we. And I had toothache that lasted over a week. We drank hot cow's milk with the hair still floating in it. It was a month when all food rotted within a day or two and I dragged my feet among the strawberries, back aching, fingers stung; I wanted to forget everything and go back home and sleep. Then the storm came. It was violent. One whole family were killed in their one-room house which was aflame within seconds; they were such a weedy lot, pitiable in some ways even before the tragedy.

It seemed to storm for days. Birds screamed their way under forbidding clouds towards shelter, cows were restlessly noisy. We were all frightened as we sat round our coffee-cups and playing-cards. Nor did the storm clear the air; it was just as sultry afterwards. And there was the funeral to attend, with burnt corpses lying in their coffins.

The old man who owned the place, and was suffering from cancer, went out with his rifle day and night and shot at imaginary apple thieves. He was mean and lonely and never talked as he paid your salary from his safe, where the notes were piled high. He was surrounded by weapons, as he was by enemies. He didn't even get on with his son; you could hear them shouting curses at each other across the grounds. The lady pickers opened tins of evil-smelling rotten fish that were supposed to be a delicacy, for a goodbye party on a Saturday night. The aquavit bottles which had been lying in cold water were soon consumed. Nobody had much to say. The two next-door ladies became really violent and swore at each other, when not being sick in the bushes. Amid the stink from the fish one of the ladies fondled me and Mother grew angry.

Somehow I fell asleep among debris, angry words and smells. Later, when I opened my eyes, I saw the ladies kissing in full view of everyone; nobody cared; what did it matter? And I still had my toothache which by now affected my whole head. I was taking aspirins all day and I was exhausted.

But I was just as wretched back in town as I had been in the country and dragged my feet on hot paving-stones, looking for a job, visiting the dentist. I had so many holes that it seemed better to take the lot away; none the less I sat day after day receiving fillings and it was still hot. The dentist was free and pretty brutal and had no time. There were long waits. We nervously eyed the door and each other. The magazines were thumbed and old, and I even read the advertisements to keep my mind off the agony of what was in store.

I only got the job because the owner was going into hospital. I often wonder how she dared to leave me in charge, for I was there for only a week before the ambulance came for her. It was the tiniest shop imaginable with a cubbyhole at the back where even I, small as I was, could only just about turn round. But there was a gas-ring, running water, a chair and a small table; and a curtain one could pull for privacy. There was no toilet, so one had to climb on the chair, squat over the sink and hope no customer would arrive. I heated up my tin box of sausages and mash and had endless cups of sweet and creamy coffee. It was dreary, the clientele meagre, poor.

And it was a drugstore, so the dirty-minded soon discovered that the formidable lady had been replaced by a girl who hardly reached up to the counter. At first it was telephone calls, nasty words, suggestions, abuses. And then they came personally for their jockstraps and rubbers and I blushed my way through the sales. Sometimes they would go so far as to play with themselves in full view of me, and I was too weak and frightened to say anything, only hoped they would finish quickly and leave.

Then the gangs of boys from the park opposite gathered in front of the shop and sometimes entered, and I lied to them, saying we didn't stock such things. But most of all I hated those coarse whispers on the telephone and what the voice at the other end really wanted. I ordered things from the factories, kept the cash in my bag, embezzled — curiously enough — very little; after all I was in charge. And once in the middle of the night I woke with a start, having forgotten to lock the door. But I was in luck. Nobody had noticed the open shop.

But to be persecuted by all the frustrated sex maniacs in that part of the city, to be on the verge of tears all the time, that was a nightmare, that was a life of fantasy filled with horror. So as soon as the owner returned I left in favour of a big store, once more in a part of the city populated by drunks, layabouts, grey, middle-of-the-road people, and of course they at once put me into the men's underwear department. I cried when I was alone behind the counter, sitting on a box of, needless to say, jockstraps. But in such a big store the customer only dared to whisper a suggestion under his breath, though eventually they fired me when in front of a male customer, tears rolling down my cheeks, I had been unable to contain my laughter when he asked — or so I thought — for a pair of moonbeam trousers. Such a relief it was.

And again I ended up in an odd corner, a mail-order business owned by an old gentleman whose office was at home. One wall was lined with grey boxes of women's underclothing, and though I took some, because he handled them so gently, I never dared wear them and wondered who could — though I looked at them every night and had my fantasies, as perhaps he did too. There was almost no work, apart from writing one letter a day and dusting the boxes, as he preferred to touch the clothes himself and pack them; but he always had to have me there as, taking his time, he stroked out every little wrinkle. I was supposed to be learning how to do it. But though worried by the strange way he looked at me as he did it, I stayed because he had a library and I started to read for the first time in my life, Tolstoy, Chekhov, Gorki, Lagerlöf, Romain Rolland, Maupassant, Zola. The only thing he asked, while I read, was that I sit in a special chair without my shoes and stockings, skirt up high, while he sat behind a desk fiddling with papers. But I would totally forget him for the words I was reading. So we were both happy. To my surprise I even got a rise in salary. Although I was quite aware of his business behind the desk, I decided to take no notice of it. I felt by now it was my lot to be pursued by lecherous men, and as long as they didn't spring at me, left me alone, it was just as well to accept it, especially with — compared to the others — a gentleman like this.

'Father's birthday. He would have been 96, 96 yes, today, and could have been 96 like other people one has known; but mercifully was not. His life would have entirely ended mine. What would have happened? No writing, no books — inconceivable.

'I used to think of him and mother daily; but writing the *Lighthouse* laid them in my mind. And now he comes back sometimes, but differently. (I believe this to be true — that I was obsessed by them both, unhealthily, and writing of them was a necessary act). He comes back now more as a contemporary. I must read him some day. I wonder if I can feel again, I hear his voice, I know this by heart?

'So the days pass and I ask myself sometimes whether one is not hypnotised, as a child by a silver globe, by life; and whether this is living. It's very quick, bright, exciting, but superficial perhaps. I should like to take the globe in my hands and feel it quietly, round, smooth, heavy, and so hold it, day after day. I will read Proust, I think. I will go backwards and forwards.

Virginia Woolf, *A Writer's Diary,* 28 November 1928

II *Toga Virilis*

Ne plus ultra

Stella's body was full of growing pains, all the seams in her dresses were bursting. She was so obviously no longer a little girl that it changed the atmosphere in the hut and she had been moved to a bunk of her own next to Jutta. It was no use protesting this time; she felt moody, lonely, unfulfilled, despite the surrounding love.

She was glad in summer when they were on the move again, up the mountain to an idyll of green pasture with a herd of cows which they were to look after for a few months. It was a grey house with a grass roof encircled by violet hills and wild flowers fighting for prominence on the slope. It had made them both smile — but what had made her dance like a child and laugh was the bed inside. Hjalmar hadn't understood at first, but her joy was so catching, spontaneous. What was so funny? The words came babbling out: I can sleep with you again. The bed monstrously filled the room, spread with animal skins, leaving no other possible place for her to sleep. He opened his arms wide and she ran to them and the warmth of his body spread to hers and suddenly there was no longer any floor, she was floating in his arms; and gently he took her face, looked at it searchingly, then kissed her lips long and softly.

She sucked his mouth; it was so hot and alive. She felt a

sudden insatiable hunger and a violent thirst, she gave herself to his mouth with such completeness that finally he pushed her away, so taken aback that he did not speak for a long time, and she in turn was so hurt by his sudden withdrawal that they took hours to reach a sense of togetherness again.

But then after their frugal supper they threw cushions and laughed and it seemed so long since they had been open with each other. She slipped her hand into his, she gazed at his far-away face and, feeling her eyes on him, he finally turned upon her such a soft brown glance that she melted again and wanted him to kiss her as before—and dared to whisper it. There was tension between them. He did nothing. He looked at her searchingly. And then she placed her lips softly on his and he took it without response, but soon his pupils clouded over and moved deep into themselves, she opened her lips and he began to feel for her with his body. But then again he drew back and put the blanket gently over them and whispered that they must stop and go to sleep. And all night they clung to each other in desperation, hearts thumping, hardly sleeping.

The daylight hours crawled. He had to take the animals to grazing areas away from the house and even the flowers paled in his absence. And when he returned they walked in wide circles that narrowed as the evening sun set low on the horizon. There was everything to say, yet nothing. Never had they been so quiet together. He watched her every move until she became self-conscious, head spinning, stomach fluttering, lighter than thistledown, yet strong as concrete. Time ceased to have any point, although she vaguely knew it was long past their bed-time. He read. Paced the floor. Smoked his pipe. Sat down with remote eyes—yet always closer than ever. And she sat with her knitting. Losing stitches. Hands slightly shaking. She felt no fatigue, but hour after hour passed. The night was a pale sky, a low sun full of the singing of migrants.

She felt him caressing her whole body as slowly she made her way to the bed. She stared down into it as if mesmerized and did not hear his question, forgetting what she had come to look for, her whole past a vague dream. Time was now, a beginning of everything. His presence set her on fire. Her legs would no longer carry her. It was hard to breathe, her head was at a standstill. And then, after an age, she heard his deliberate movements, the scraping of the chair, the rustling of his clothes, the firm slow steps — every sound heightened, almost deafening, the very air standing still in this island of a universe.

The goddesses of love were their guardian angels, she could hear them laying their plots and Eros sharpening his spear. Every gate was flung open for the celebration of the meeting of their bodies, she was weightless in his arms, she was being swept up to the brightest star in the cloud of stars, and though so difficult to be coherent as they searched deep in their bodies for each other, she dimly thought this had always been what was missing, this flaming heat of a June day, these volcanoes bursting in the sea, this rawness in which she was born, so new, so total, so painfully for the first time, these arms and legs which opened to another body which was his, yet as much hers.

They would now scale heights that were impossible alone. Three magic words, whispered in her ear, as the world erupted into a glistening jewel; and as the night grew old, they lay together complete, gently rocked to sleep in the young moon's arms. They were as rich as all the heavens in the firmament and man had become an angel.

'The heavens are a spirit and a vapour in which we live just like a bird in time. Not only the stars and the moon constitute the heavens, but also these are stars in us, and these which are in us and which we do not see constitute the heavens also ... The firmament is twofold, that of the heavens and that of the bodies ... Man's strength comes from the upper firmament and all his power lies in it. As the former may be weak or strong, so, too, is the firmament of the body.' Paracelsus

I still only functioned. I was that many kilos of flesh, had eyes made of stones that didn't see, ears that were deaf to stars and dew and all that was myself, and I lay buried in something very black. My sturdy legs carried me about with no idea of direction, my arms were weak and bore weak useless things from one place to another. I was walled in and knew nothing of it.

I certainly wasn't aware of you then, although you lived in me — which I was only to realize so many years later. But if we didn't share this experience, let me at least try to tell you. I just don't know how many days after Christmas it was — was I sixteen or seventeen perhaps? — when we four girls were seated in the room gossiping, totally unprepared for what was going to happen. Yes, that I can honestly say; to this day they would testify to the reality of the situation. Picture a very ordinary room with its four solid walls, a shabby Christmas tree in a corner, all fairly poor, without taste or hope. We felt as gloomy as the place and our talk was the talk of children; the only reason for being together was that we were all pupils in a dramatic school of an eccentric character. None of us paid much. I paid not a penny.

We were supposed to be talented. Though we had hardly grasped this point, we were eagerly grasping the affection and security which the teacher gave us all. We had enjoyed so little of it before. This was luck; and though cynically you could say that this teacher liked little girls, all he did was roll his eyes quietly at us from time to time with his hands firmly in his pockets — which made us laugh.

The street noises were shut off because the flat was on the third floor and turned inwards to another apartment. The light was dimmish. The candles in the tree had long ago guttered down. We were full of scraps of ham and mustard and bread and coffee and most probably a cake. We were all fairly buried small people with not many thoughts in our heads, and I was perhaps the most buried in a world of no shadows where all seemed blacker than black.

And suddenly there was light.

I shall try to do that most impossible thing, to communicate that light. My sky could not have been more overcast; you would never think that the smallest ray of sunshine could filter through that blanket which I had spun so carelessly over my head. But then came this light, this overwhelming light, that flooded everything, that swamped the room. From what heavens was it perhaps just a spark? But a spark which stayed and healed, coming with a suddenness that overpowered me and filled me with radiant energy. It was at least ten times as strong as broad daylight, it was like looking into the sun without being blinded, and there was no heat, and I was burning within it for how many seconds, minutes, no one could or can answer that question, then or now. It was infinity. It might have been a second. But its powers have remained and worked within me. Is that how conversions are made? Perhaps. Or just great changes.

Physically my body seemed to disappear; my friends, myself, were imaged in a mirror seen from afar. The light was just white, perhaps slightly milky and of limitless depth; the room faded behind it, sounds and smells did not exist in this light. In that moment the world had come to a halt for me. I could see backwards into the blackness with the utmost clarity, into my half-animal being, the chaos, my lostness, the web of ignorance that enshrouded me, into all of which I seemed to be rushing, hell-bent on destroying myself. All those poor years I had looked outside for consolation; now I was to see that the greatest of acts was to look inwards to find the treasures. Without knowing it I could suddenly face my own darkness and drive my black raven out and instead go in search of the white dove. I could see, with my vision, without words, that all the poisons would be draining out of me and I saw that blackness as if it were stickily painted over the contours of the earth in which I had been wallowing without awareness of it.

So, apparently, the light had been on my face. Someone cried when I came back to the gloomy room, now even gloomier, but I was radiant within and didn't know what to think or do or how to explain. Yet I knew I had been touched—but by what? I had not fainted. I had become, it seemed, slightly rigid, eyes wide and remote. And if the others had not actually seen the light in the room, it had cast its shadow on to my bewildered face, which it had luminously painted.

From that moment the repairs began. Yes, Stella, it was a most amazing, hair-raising experience, and I'm glad to have been able to tell it at last, though how could I possibly do it justice? Words are puny and few, my brain small in comparison, for what I glimpsed was truth, genius, God, love, call it all those things and many more, provided I also call it the most real and most good thing I have ever known. That is where my life started, Stella, and all was changed, and I was open to everything at last.

'To savour all the stars, all the heavens, it is enough for a man to taste a crust of bread.' Paracelsus